The Postman's Fiancée

Also by Denis Thériault

The Peculiar Life of a Lonely Postman
The Boy Who Belonged to the Sea

The Postman's Fiancée

Denis Thériault

Translated by John Cullen

ONEWORLD

A Oneworld Book

First published in North America, Great Britain and
Australia by Oneworld Publications, 2017

Originally published in French as *La fiancée du facteur* by
XYZ Publishing, 2016
Copyright © Denis Thériault, 2016
Translation copyright © John Cullen, 2017

Published by agreement with Allied Authors Agency, Belgium

Illustrations by Nomoco

The moral right of Denis Thériault to be identified as the
Author of this work has been asserted by him in accordance
with the Copyright, Designs, and Patents Act 1988

ISBN 978-1-78607-113-2
ISBN 978-1-78607-114-9 (eBook)

Printed and bound in Great Britain by Clays Ltd, St Ives plc

This is a work of fiction. While, as in all fiction, the literary perceptions
and insights are based on experience, all names, characters,
places, and incidents either are products of the author's imagination
or are used fictitiously.

Oneworld Publications
10 Bloomsbury Street
London WC1B 3SR
England

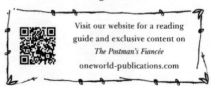

Visit our website for a reading
guide and exclusive content on
The Postman's Fiancée
oneworld-publications.com

The Postman's Fiancée

Tania, the fastest waitress this side of Mexico. Two *plats du jour* for table four – two *poutines* and a Hawaiian pizza for table seven – one cottage pie at the counter – a tomato sandwich for Mr Grandpré, table two...Tania made sure to satisfy all those hungry mouths diligently and courteously, but she didn't stop there; she went above and beyond the requirements of her job, as if driven by the ambition of elevating the waitress's profession to the level of art. You had to see her, moving with such agility, shuttling light-footed, even while loaded down with dishes, between the kitchen and the narrow aisles in the dining room. Adroitly juggling plates and glasses, she'd clear a table and set it for you in less time than it took to say, 'Would you like to see the menu?' Then she'd spring behind the counter like a gazelle and pour coffee with sure, graceful movements. Watching Tania float about that way was like seeing an acrobatic ballet danced to a soundtrack of masticating jaws and clinking silverware. Rarely in the history of the Montreal restaurant business had patrons been privileged to admire a waitress so lively, so radiant, at work. People often asked Tania how she managed to be everywhere at once, and always attentive. Some attributed her extraordinary efficiency to her German genes, for Tania was, in fact, from Bavaria; she'd spent her childhood in the Munich area, and if you listened closely, you could hear a slight German accent. Others suspected her of practising some sort of magic or of being blessed with the gift of ubiquity, suspicions that made Tania laugh. Because for all that, the explanation of her daily performance was quite simple: she loved her job. She liked the ambience in the Madelinot, she respected her customers and she made it her duty to satisfy them.

Tania had arrived in Montreal five years before, ostensibly to attend university and perfect her French – her second language, which she'd learned in high school – but the real reason for her coming was to be with a boy she'd met on the Internet. The boy had disappointed her; the city, however, was very much to her taste, and she'd decided to settle there. Perhaps Tania wouldn't be a waitress all her life. At some point in the future she'd probably complete her studies, even though boredom had caused her to abandon them for the time being. But that wasn't a pressing concern; for the moment, working at the Madelinot gave her a sensation of happy equilibrium, a feeling of harmony with the universe.

Tania Schumpf lived on a peaceful street in the Villeray neighbourhood. Her apartment was small but stylish, painted in warm colours and furnished with a fireplace. Tania spent pleasant evenings there, reading novels, watching movies, daydreaming in complete tranquillity. She seldom went out, and then solely on Saturday evenings with her confidante

He came through the door every day at noon, impeccable in his postman's uniform. He was tall, rather thin and not exactly handsome, but his gentle eyes and timid smile made Tania go weak inside. His name was Bilodo.

He didn't know that Tania was in love with him. He was a shy young man, as shy as she was, if not shyer.

Whatever the weather, he would infallibly show up on the stroke of noon, and Tania, a punctual girl, loved that regularity. He wasn't like the other postmen from the Postal Depot, the nearby post-sorting facility, who would come in for lunch in noisy packs and try to chat her up and tell her dirty jokes. Bilodo was different. He rarely joined his boorish colleagues. He preferred to sit at the counter, where he'd eat his meal without disturbing a soul. Tania found his presence reassuring.

After dessert, Bilodo would turn his attention to his favourite pastime. He'd take an exercise notebook and some pens out of his bag and devote himself to the practice of calligraphy, the delicate art of beautiful handwriting. Tania would observe him out of the corner of her eye while he assiduously copied certain portions of the menu or a few lines from a newspaper article. Bilodo had long, nimble fingers, and Tania never tired of watching his pen as it turned and glided in their grasp. One of Tania's duties required her to inscribe the menu of the day on a slate each morning, a task she performed with great care, writing in her prettiest hand and hoping that Bilodo would notice. Having done some research on calligraphy, she'd draw up his bill in Uncial, a script he seemed to favour, and sign it with a 'Tania' embellished with discreet flourishes. Bilodo must have appreciated her work because he always left her a large tip.

Ever since Bilodo came into her life, Tania had had the impression that her bed was growing a little bigger each night, becoming as vast and frosty as the Gobi Desert. When the twittering of the birds awakened her in the morning, his smile was the first thing she thought of, and at night, before she fell asleep, her last thoughts were of him, of his pianist's fingers, so skilful in manipulating the pen; and she would blush, imagining them exploring her body... During the quiet periods when the restaurant was empty and she'd be standing idly near the till, her reveries would focus on him, and it was because of him that she'd dash into the ladies' room at ten to twelve to check her hair and refresh her make-up. The image she saw in the mirror left her dissatisfied. Tania found her chin too long, her breasts too small. She was sorry she wasn't sexier, but she guessed Bilodo knew how to look past appearances. She made an effort to compensate for the ordinariness of her charms by being abundantly kind. When it was time for dessert, she always served him a double portion of lemon tart.

He was hiding something, Tania's intuition told her. Was there some tragedy buried in his past? Had some great misfortune befallen him? As Tania engaged in such speculations, it was borne in upon her that she knew almost nothing about him. Nonetheless, she did know one thing, a fact of paramount importance: Bilodo was a bachelor. Tania's knowledge of this was due to his postal colleagues, who often teased him on the subject. How did Bilodo occupy his heart? What did he do with his nights? Tania could happily imagine him leading a monastic existence dedicated to calligraphy, saving himself physically and spiritually for the fortunate pilgrimess who would know how to find the pathway to his soul – a role for which Tania considered herself eminently qualified. But what about him? Did he feel anything for her? Tania felt she had grounds for believing that she didn't leave him indifferent – otherwise, why did he always sit at the counter, close to her? But the truth was that she couldn't be sure of anything, given the chronic timidity that muzzled them both. Should she look upon Bilodo's smile as an invitation, or was he just being polite? Since she was unable to make a conclusive assessment, Tania confined herself to uneasy suspense. Afraid of scaring Bilodo away, she was waiting for him to make the first move.

She'd been waiting like that for nearly six months, and the strange status quo might have continued ad infinitum, had Fate not suddenly intervened, wearing a grimacing mask and bringing death to rue des Hêtres.

It was a stormy day, the last day of August. Shortly before noon, the sky, having grown heavier all morning long, had finally burst, discharging rain in torrents and filling the gutters to overflowing. The elements were just beginning to calm down when Tania, busy at her work, heard the sound of a passing ambulance. A quick glance at her watch revealed that it was already ten past twelve, which surprised her, because this was the first time that Bilodo had ever deviated from the chronometric exactness of his arrival. Then Ulysse, a homeless itinerant frequently to be seen in the Madelinot, burst into the restaurant. In great agitation, he shouted that an accident had just taken place: someone had been run over and killed, by a truck, not far away, further down on rue des Hêtres.

Aware that Bilodo's postal route included that very street, Tania became alarmed. When she demanded more precise facts from Ulysse, he reported that the victim was a regular customer at the restaurant and confirmed that some postmen were on the scene. Tania's legs buckled. She was assailed by the terrible certainty that Bilodo had just been snatched away from her, that it was all over before it had even begun. Then Ulysse revealed that the dead man was 'the guy with the beard and the red flower'. Only one person fitted that description, and Tania began to breathe again, appalled to learn that the accident victim was Gaston Grandpré, a customer she was fond of, but above all relieved to know that Bilodo had been spared.

Bilodo came in around quarter past one, closely followed by his colleague Robert, who worked in post collection. Tania's joy at seeing the young postman unharmed was so keen that she nearly flung herself into his arms. There were bloodstains on Bilodo's uniform. Robert, a great talker, was happy to explain that they'd witnessed the accident. It had happened right before their eyes, in the pouring rain, in front of a postbox the collector was hurriedly emptying of its contents, and he reported that Grandpré had dashed out of his apartment building and into the deluge, rushing to post a letter. He'd run across the street, failed to see the truck bearing down on him, and BANG! The poor man was already breathing his last when they reached his side, and he'd died in their arms.

Bilodo looked shaken. With tragic eyes, he gazed at the empty place near the window where Grandpré had been wont to sit. Tania shared his affliction. She was going to miss the deceased man. She would regret Gaston Grandpré's kindness, his refined sense of humour. He was a literature professor with the dishevelled look of a mad genius, and every day since she'd started working at the Madelinot, he'd come in to eat his perennial sandwich, wearing a red carnation stuck in his buttonhole, and before leaving he'd plant the flower in the sugar bowl – an odd little ritual with which Tania had graciously complied. It was awful, what had happened to Mr Grandpré, but if she had to choose, it was better that he was the one dead rather than Bilodo...She caught herself thinking such thoughts and felt a little ashamed.

That night Tania dreamt about Gaston Grandpré, just after the accident, as he lay on Beech Street in the pouring rain. Except that it wasn't Grandpré at all, but Bilodo, covered with blood and breathing his last on the flooded asphalt. With one trembling hand, Bilodo pulled out the red carnation that adorned the buttonhole in his postman's jacket and offered it to Tania, imploring her not to forget him – and then she woke up, frightened by what turned out to have been only a nightmare.

Reconnecting with reality, Tania remembered that Bilodo was alive and well. She switched on her bedside lamp and simultaneously experienced something like an interior illumination: interpreting her dream as a portent, she was suddenly aware of the fragility of life, of its terrible brevity. Then it was that Tania realized she could procrastinate no longer: 'What are you waiting for, Tania Schumpf? If you want Bilodo to belong to you, hurry up and take the initiative before it's too late,' she railed at herself, feeling the urgency to act. Tania's heart went out to Gaston Grandpré, to whom she believed she owed this revelation. She begged his pardon for preferring his death to Bilodo's and thanked him for having contributed, by his passing, to opening her eyes.

The next day, on her way to the Madelinot, Tania bought a red carnation at the florist's, and when she got to the restaurant, she planted the flower in the sugar bowl on Grandpré's favourite table as a posthumous homage. 'Take the initiative, right. But how?' she wondered, contemplating the solitary carnation. How could she build a bridge to Bilodo? What means could she use to draw them closer to each other?

That question quickly became obsessive, haunting Tania's every waking hour. Luckily, it didn't take her too long to find the answer; an opportunity presented itself when Bilodo developed a sudden passion for Asian poetry. One September day around noon, he showed Tania a book titled *Traditional Haiku of the Seventeenth Century* and spoke enthusiastically about those charming little poems, which contained only seventeen syllables. As the days passed, it appeared obvious that Japanese lyrical art was

3

Image reflected
in butterfly's eye:
peak of a distant mountain

As this fall day dawned
the mirror I peered into
held my father's face

Occasional clouds
offer a respite
to those in love with the moon

Under the wild grass
warriors' wild dreams
still restlessly quivering

The first of these four haiku was written by Buson,
the second by Kijo, and the last two by Bashō, all
classic masters of the genre. Composed of three lines
– two of five syllables and one of seven – and a total
of seventeen syllables, each haiku sought to juxta-
pose the immutable and the ephemeral. Restrained
and precise, a good haiku had to contain a reference
to nature (*kigo*) or to a reality that was not exclu-
sively human. The art of the haiku was the art of the
instantaneous, of the detail; a haiku was a concrete

poem, making its appeal to the senses rather than to ideas.

Captivated by the apparent simplicity of this concept, Tania tried to compose some haiku. It didn't take her long to find out that such compositions were far from easy. She brought an anthology of Japanese haiku to the Madelinot and had Bilodo read the ones she considered the most beautiful. He was agreeably surprised to discover that Tania shared his interest in haiku, but he refused to show her the ones he wrote, using the excuse that it was a personal matter. Nevertheless, Tania had succeeded in getting his attention. It was a start.

Tania downloaded a selection of Japanese songs, and every day at five to twelve, she pressed play. After learning the basics of *ikebana* and origami, she decorated the restaurant with floral arrangements and populated it with pretty little animals made of folded paper. These manoeuvres had no apparent effect on Bilodo, but they didn't escape the notice of his colleague Robert, who had guessed some time previously that Tania had a crush on the young postman.

One day at lunch, Robert took her aside and said, 'I have to admit, I don't understand.'

'Don't understand what?' asked Tania cautiously, for she was wary of this particular postal worker.

Conceited and loud, Robert reigned over the boisterous pack of postmen, whom he ceaselessly regaled with updated tales of his female conquests and fabulous sexual exploits. Believing himself to be a kind of Casanova, he had undertaken to woo Tania with increasingly frequent insinuations and innuendo, to which she was careful not to reply.

'I don't understand what you see in that boy,' Robert explained, gesturing towards Bilodo, who was sitting at the counter, bent over his writing. 'Why waste your time on such an oddball?'

Tania shot him an icy look. The thing that irritated her most about Robert was the disgraceful way he treated Bilodo. Even though he proclaimed himself to be his colleague's best friend, Robert actually never missed a chance to make fun of him. He scoffed at Bilodo for his persistent celibacy and had taken upon himself the role of go-between, in which he tried to mate Bilodo with anything that moved; he registered him with online dating services and, without his knowledge, posted crude personal ads in his name on social media. Robert even went so far as to distort Bilodo's very name, rechristening him 'Libido', a supreme irony with which his fellow postmen had a field day. More than anyone, Tania understood how he must have felt when they called him that, for as a child she'd had to endure a similar situation. Schumpf, originally an Alsatian family name, sounded strange to Bavarian ears and was transformed by her schoolmates into something more familiar: Schlumpf, the German word for one of the little blue humanoids called *Schtroumpfs* in French and 'Smurfs' in English. Tania Schlumpf, Tania Smurf! This nickname, along with its diminutive *Schlumpfine* – 'Smurfette' – had cast a shadow over her childhood, and when she saw Bilodo subjected to similarly absurd nicknaming, she sympathized with him, feeling closer to him than ever.

'What you need is a man worthy of the name,' Robert went on.

'And you call yourself his friend?' Tania asked indignantly.

'Friendship has nothing to do with it. This is all about the burning desire I feel for you, my lovely Tania,' said Robert salaciously.

Hardly concealing her contempt, Tania ignored him.

All autumn long, she continued to perform variations on the Japanese theme; she placed a bonsai plant on the counter and persuaded Mr Martinez, the chef, to add some sushi dishes to the menu. For Halloween, she dressed as a geisha, naturally.

'*Konnichi wa*,' she said, bowing to the astonished Bilodo when he came in.

He bowed in return and complimented her on her beautiful costume. Then, as soon as he'd finished his lunch, he plunged into his haiku. This tepid reaction disappointed Tania, who had taken great pains with her outfit – she'd spent two hours just on her make-up and hairdo.

'Nice try, Madam Butterfly,' said Robert mockingly when Tania, unsteady on her wooden clogs, came to warm up his coffee. 'You'd do better coming home with me. I'll show you my big samurai sword.'

'I'd rather commit hara-kiri!'

Robert insisted, evoking the prospect of a Hiroshima of carnal pleasure, but Tania hurried away to bid farewell to Bilodo, who was leaving already: '*Sayonara*, my love!' she said, to herself.

> Tick-tock goes the clock
> marking out the hours
> my heart beats for only you

Tania shredded the poem and threw it into the fireplace, where it went up in smoke. She sighed. Was Bilodo suffering from the same creative anxieties? He didn't look like it; every afternoon, he applied himself to his own haiku with imperturbable discipline, apparently exempt from writer's block. Although flattered by Tania's ongoing interest in his work, he still refused to let her see what he was writing and hastily shut his notebook as soon as she got too close. Thoroughly intrigued by this mystery, Tania wondered whether Bilodo's poems might not contain references to her, and was all the more curious to have a look at them – and so it occurred to her to start a *renku*.

It was while reading a history of Japanese poetry that she'd come across the term *renku*. This was a poetic tradition that went back to the literary contests held in bygone days in the Imperial Court of Japan. The result of a collaborative effort on the part of several authors, a *renku* ('linked verses') comprised a sequence of haiku in which each one, each link, responded to the link preceding it. The prospect of exchanging poems like that with her own true love had immediately enthralled Tania. Bilodo, she believed, would be unable to resist the allure of such an experience. But in order to succeed, she still had to begin the process by presenting him with a first haiku worthy of achieving her purpose – and there was the rub:

> All along Beech Street
> only maple leaves
> blowing about in the wind

> Dry leaves of autumn
> blowing in the wind
> not a beech leaf among them

> If trees on Beech Street
> are for the most part maples
> this is not my fault

> To beech, not to beech
> how important can it be
> trees couldn't care less

> Autumn on Beech Street

> the wind – the maples
> what a brimming crock of shit!

Tania tore up those preposterous haiku. Was there anything more horrible than the sensation of going round in circles inside your own head? Her whole being aspired to *wabi* (sober beauty in harmony with nature), but it was as though the age-old virtues of *sabi* (simplicity, serenity) were refusing to penetrate her. How was she to reach the subtle equilibrium between *fueki* (the permanent, the eternity that extends beyond us) and *ryuko* (the fleeting, the ephemeral that passes through us), those indispensable elements of a good haiku? Where could you learn to write that type of thing?

'Stop wasting your time writing poems,' her friend Noémie advised her. They were sitting at the bar in a pub on rue Notre-Dame. 'If you're sure this boy's the right one for you, stop thinking about it, and full speed ahead!'

Noémie was Tania's oldest friend in Montreal. She too was a waitress and worked in a café in the Quartier Latin where Tania had also been employed during her first year at university. Pretty and extroverted, Noémie possessed the kind of mischievous smile that captivated men, an advantage she didn't fail to make the very most of: more than once, Tania had been obliged to help her extricate herself from complex erotic situations involving several concurrent lovers. Nevertheless, although the two of them were very close, it was only recently that Tania had dared to confide to Noémie the tender feelings that Bilodo aroused in her.

'Are you waiting for some other little minx to snatch him away from you? Get him in a corner and put him through the wringer.'

Tania shrugged. That was easy for a sexual electromagnet like Noémie to say, but for the timid Tania Schumpf, it was a different matter entirely. The method Noémie was recommending seemed excessively bold to Tania; to provoke Bilodo that way was to risk ruining everything. When dealing with such a sensitive boy, wasn't it important to proceed instead with infinite delicacy?

'If you insist on subtlety, I can give you a love philtre,' Noémie proposed. 'My Haitian neighbour concocts it. Three drops in your postman's soup will do the trick.'

But Tania declined this offer, persuaded that the only fitting magic for her purposes was the magic of words, preferably in sets of seventeen syllables.

Tania awoke on the sofa at four in the morning, slightly bewildered. Straining to produce a decent haiku, she'd filled page after page, scrawling, crossing out, counting and recounting syllables and then crossing out everything again, until she'd finally fallen asleep amidst an erg of torn paper. Outside, the first snow of winter was falling in lazy flakes illuminated by the pallid light of the streetlamps. Tania hurriedly slipped on her coat and went out. With childish pleasure, she trod the white carpet that covered the pavement. The city was deserted, immaculate. As she walked through the snow, Tania opened her mouth, trying to catch a drifting flake that landed on her nose instead...and suddenly she knew what she had to write. Wouldn't it be enough to stick to the natural simplicity that had so generously inspired the old masters?

Tania ran home, and in less than ten minutes, she composed this:

> Neophyte parachutist
> an early snowflake
> dissolves on my nose

Wabi – sabi – fueki – ryuko: they were all there. It was no work of genius, but it might suffice.

Tania copied out her haiku onto a sheet of fancy paper and the following afternoon presented the poem to Bilodo, who seemed greatly impressed. In gratitude, he promised to write a poem for her very soon. Tania gloated discreetly; her plan was working, a *renku* had been born. All she had to do was await Bilodo's poetic response.

Tania had no inkling that her patience would be so sorely tested.

4

It was already April when Tania, clearing Bilodo's place at the counter while he was in the toilets, found a folded piece of paper with her name written on it. 'At last,' she whispered, presuming that this was the haiku that had been promised her. She'd been waiting for that poem for weeks, and then months, with vanishing hope, and in the end she'd assumed that Bilodo had forgotten. And look, all at once her patience was rewarded. Tania unfolded the paper, burning to read what had taken Bilodo a whole winter to compose:

> Some flowers, it seems,
> are seven years a-blooming
> For a long time now
> I have longed to say to you
> all the love words in my heart

To Tania's ears, it was as if a choir of angels had intoned a *Gloria*. Trembling with joy that bordered on ecstasy, she went and stationed herself outside the men's toilets, from which Bilodo soon emerged, taken aback at the sight of her. Tania thanked him for the marvellous surprise and confessed, her cheeks aflame, that the feeling was mutual. Bilodo gazed dumbfounded at the poem Tania was pressing

23

against her throbbing breast. 'I have to go,' he stammered. Gauging how much courage it must have cost so shy a man to make such a declaration of love, Tania required nothing more, for the time being; and while Bilodo, visibly upset, was leaving the restaurant, she favoured him with her most radiant smile.

Tania spent the rest of the afternoon in a state of weightlessness. She kept on rereading the remarkable poem – five lines long instead of three – that had just magnified her life. Her recent research enabled her to recognize that the verses were written in an ancient Japanese poetic form: *tanka*, haiku's august ancestor. A tanka was made up of two parts: the first, a tercet of seventeen syllables, was in fact a haiku, to which a second part was added, a distich – two lines, each containing seven syllables – that responded to the first part and gave the stanza a new direction. In contrast with haiku, which spoke to the senses and tended to involve the observation of nature, tanka dealt with such noble themes as death and love. Tania understood why Bilodo had taken so long to write his poem: unwilling to settle for declaring his feelings in a simple haiku, he'd taken the trouble to explore that other poetic form, dedicated to the expression of complex emotions.

Afloat on a pink cloud, Tania spent her evening creating a tanka that would respond to Bilodo's and convey, with a judiciously calibrated mixture of passion and modesty, her desire to give herself to him:

My heart has been yours
for an even longer time
Yours, waiting for you
The fruit that slowly ripens
tastes all the more delicious

It was almost noon, and Tania was waiting for Bilodo, her tanka in her pocket, when the postal workers showed up, led by Robert, who was himself preceded by a swollen nose. Tania had noted the swelling the previous day; it was obviously the result of a blow, but Robert had been evasive. When Tania complimented him on the remarkable colouration of his honker, Robert, loquacious as ever, had declared that she should rather compliment his attacker, Bilodo. Having recently witnessed some violent arguments between the two men, Tania wasn't so surprised. The reason for their dispute remained obscure: it seemed that Bilodo had risen up, and not a moment too soon, against the endless indignities inflicted on him by his co-worker. If Bilodo had gone so far as to strike Robert, it could only have been in reaction to some particularly outrageous insult. In any case, Tania was certainly not going to feel sorry for Bilodo's tormenter.

'Tell me something, Tania,' Robert said unctuously. 'Yesterday I saw you read a note Libido had left on the counter. It was a love poem, wasn't it?'

Tania dared not ask him how he knew that, nor how Bilodo's tanka could possibly interest him. 'None of your business,' she replied, preparing to beat a quick retreat.

But Robert reached inside his coat, took out a sheet of paper, and held it under her nose. 'Was it this poem?'

A scalding shudder ran through Tania's body. Robert was talking about Bilodo's tanka, many copies of which, he informed her, were circulating at the Depot. A shocked Tania listened as Robert explained that the poem hadn't been meant for her, that its intended recipient was a Guadeloupian woman named Ségolène with whom Bilodo corresponded, and with whom he was mightily taken: 'When Libido told me he wanted to give you a copy, I found the notion immoral. I tried to stop him, and that's why he punched me.'

A deathly silence had fallen upon the restaurant. The other customers, who'd been following the conversation, looked at Tania and felt terribly sorry for her. It was then, on the stroke of noon, that Bilodo came in. His arrival was greeted by the sniggers of the postmen. Determined at all costs to avoid meeting his eyes, Tania ran and hid in the kitchen, shaken to the core, her back against the wall. She could hear the postmen on the other side, heckling Bilodo and roaring, 'Ségolène! In your sloop! Sail me back to Guadeloupe!' Tania took Bilodo's tanka out of her apron pocket and read it again, trying to understand. So this poem, and all the others – had he written them for this Ségolène person? The thought stunned her, and she let herself slide down the wall. Turning his head away from the stove and seeing her like that, Mr Martinez became alarmed; as he lifted her from the floor, he asked her to tell him what was wrong, but the stupefied Tania barely heard him. Why had Bilodo let her read that poem? Was this a nasty practical joke dreamt up by the postmen? Was she paying the price for some idiotic bet? Seething with anger, Tania grabbed a tray loaded with food and left the kitchen.

Bilodo was seated at the counter, looking wretched. Tania ignored him and brought the other postmen their meals. Robert's ostentatious contrition didn't deceive her; she could feel him enjoying her defeat. She served the postal workers without flinching and then went to take Bilodo's order, so icy she could have sunk the *Titanic*. What would he have? Another sitting duck, like her? A guinea pig to test out his poems on? Bilodo told her she was mistaken and asked to speak to her in private, but Tania replied that it wouldn't be worth the trouble. She crumpled up the fraudulent tanka and threw it at him. 'Here's your poem, Libido,' she said scathingly.

There followed a burst of applause, for Tania was not without supporters. Bilodo stammered that it was none of his doing, that she had never been meant to see the poem. So he didn't deny having written the tanka for someone else, which Tania considered equivalent to a confession. Refusing to hear any more about it, she commanded him to go somewhere else and find another victim – an order punctuated by fresh applause. It was too much for Tania, who once again ran to the kitchen for refuge. Bilodo wanted to follow her, but Mr Martinez – 130 hostile kilos, not counting the kitchen knife in his hand – blocked the postman's way and advised him to make himself scarce. Bilodo chose to comply. Tania heard him slam the restaurant door. Devastated, she sagged against Mr Martinez's shoulder and cried her eyes out.

'How could you let yourself be manipulated like that, Tania Schumpf?' she said in self-reproach that evening, seeking to drown her sorrows in a bottle of Chardonnay. So Bilodo's feelings for her, the feelings she'd thought she perceived – they'd been only fantasies? How could her sublime love story have turned into a horror film so suddenly? Tania was certain of only one thing: she was suffering horribly, from Bilodo's duplicity, from his cynicism – but the most piercing of all her torments came with an overwhelming realization: 'I still love him.' For so she did, as absurd as that was. In spite of all the wrong Bilodo was doing her, she continued to love him. 'But he loves someone else!' she cried to herself in despair, and it was as though a knife had been thrust through her heart.

What was he doing at that moment? Was he writing to his Guadeloupian woman? Dreaming about her?

It was only out of her sense of duty that Tania went to work the following day. Twelve o'clock passed with no sign of Bilodo, who dared not show himself. Better for him. The other customers, having witnessed the previous day's psychodrama, treated Tania like a delicate porcelain piece the merest impact could pulverize. People felt sorry for her, which only further stung her wounded pride.

The crowd from the Postal Depot invaded the restaurant at ten past twelve. 'Your fiancé won't be here today, my poor Tania,' Robert announced. 'He called in sick.'

Tania stoically took the postmen's orders and passed them on to the kitchen. Then she saw Ulysse signalling to her from the back of the dining room. The peripatetic Ulysse was a veteran of the war in Afghanistan, in which he had suffered a head wound and from which he'd returned much diminished mentally. Like his illustrious namesake, he was a wanderer, roaming around in the subway, travelling from one station to another, trying to get back to his home, whose address he had unfortunately forgotten. Ulysse sometimes sank into paranoia and thought he was being pursued by a Cyclops disguised as a policeman, but he always behaved like a perfect gentleman with Tania, whom he worshipped, taking her for a Greek goddess.

Concealing her troubles, Tania went to him and

asked to be told the wishes of Ithaca's exiled king. But the latter didn't want to talk about the menu: 'I saw everything, noble daughter of Zeus. I was here the day before yesterday, and I watched that dirty swine' – here Ulysse paused in his whispering and thrust an accusatory chin in the direction of Robert, two tables away – 'carry out his dastardly scheme. I saw him seize on a moment of inattention, when you were in the kitchen and the postman was in the toilets, to place on the counter the infernal poem through which your honour was tarnished.'

'Thank you, Ulysse,' said Tania, lining up the offending postal worker in her sights.

Everything appeared in a new light. It was all a plot, engineered by Robert. Bilodo was innocent: he'd tried to explain, but she'd been deaf to him. A wave of shame took Tania's breath away at the memory of how despicably she had accused and insulted him. What must he think of her?

So this fine mess had come to her courtesy of Mr Robert. The reason why was obvious: by inducing Tania to believe the tanka was meant for her, he was killing two birds with one stone – punishing Tania for rejecting his advances, and avenging himself on Bilodo for having punched him. Itching with an urgent desire to annihilate Robert, Tania brought the postmen their meals. She placed their daily bread before each of them apart from Robert, and then, serving him last, she coolly poured his plate of spaghetti on his head. Robert shrieked and leaped up, overturning his chair. 'What's wrong with you, you stupid bitch?' he yelped, throwing off spurts of Bolognese sauce.

'I know what you did,' Tania told him.

In a biting tone, Tania forbade Robert ever to reappear in the Madelinot, at least not when she was there; then she went to get her coat from the employees' cloakroom. When she returned to the dining room, Robert was cleaning himself off as well as he could with paper towels. 'You have no right to treat me like this,' he declared. 'I did it only for your own good.'

'My own good?' she blurted out, astonished by such cheek.

'I wanted to warn you. The Guadeloupian woman – I didn't make her up. Libido's apartment is papered with the poems he sends to her. He's really crazy about that girl.'

Dizzy from the fresh knife wound in her guts, Tania left the restaurant. Once she was outside, she paused a moment to pull herself together, then marched down the pavement like a soldier. She knew where Bilodo lived, not far away on rue des Hêtres, because on a few occasions, unbeknownst to him, she'd followed him home. What did she hope would happen? Was she going to offer him her excuses? Repair the damage done? The closer she got to Bilodo's place, the more slowly she walked, and in the end she remained immobile in front of his house, unable to take the first step up the exterior staircase. For the problem remained unresolved: he loved another woman.

It was a comfort to know that Bilodo had played no conscious part in Robert's scheme, but his heart belonged nonetheless to that Guadeloupian, about whom Tania knew nothing. And so she went away, bent under the burden of an ineluctable fate.

5

Tania confronted the spring with clenched teeth. She made an effort to forget Bilodo, but her walks inevitably led her to the foot of that staircase she dared not climb. Sometimes in the evening, standing there on the pavement, she would stare at the lighted rectangle of his window in the hope of seeing something, if only a fleeting silhouette, move behind it.

Working at the Madelinot grew difficult for her. The delicious anticipation of Bilodo's daily appearances had given way to a tormenting void. The restaurant's atmosphere, heavy with the memory of her shame, weighed on her, and in spite of the loyalty she believed she owed Mr Martinez, Tania quit her job at the end of May.

Wondering what to do with her life, she considered the possibility of going back to Bavaria, and then she thought about finishing her bachelor's degree, as her father so fervently desired her to do. Instead she found a waitressing job at the Petit Malin (the 'smart aleck'), a brasserie in the Plateau neighbourhood. Tania soon realized that her new work wasn't going to quench her thirst for change, and in June she took a lover. He was a handsome, sporty young man who introduced her to kitesurfing and tennis, but she quickly tired of his mediocre intellect and dumped him, with relief, in July. Shortly afterwards, Tania felt an irresistible urge to move house. At the end of a search for new lodgings she rented a place in the suburbs, a modern apartment she planned to refurnish when she moved in at the end of September – provided she survived that long, because all these alterations in her way of living, carried out with the express purpose of driving Bilodo from her mind, instead only underlined his absence and made her miss him more. Wishing to help her friend get through this difficult moment, Noémie strove to find ways to distract her; she took her shopping and accompanied her to films or fashionable nightspots. Appreciative of Noémie's efforts, and feeling obliged to put on a brave face, Tania pretended to be enjoying herself, but the truth was that her soul was slowly wilting away. Nothing seemed capable of halting that internal withering, and when summer arrived in triumph, Tania, unable to savour its pleasures, preferred to shut herself up indoors, watching her favourite films on loop while stuffing herself with ice cream and wondering, twenty times a day, what Bilodo was doing, what he was thinking about.

Sometimes she had the sensation that she was slipping into madness. In agitated moments, she would give herself over to frenetic bouts of housekeeping, but then she'd subside into apathy. Aware that she had the advantage of proximity, that her rival was practically on the other side of the world, she would exhort herself to use that advantage to get her claws into Bilodo...but then she'd watch another movie. On some mornings she'd wake up in a warlike frame of mind and decide to fly to the West Indies and face the Guadeloupian woman in single combat...but then common sense would return, she'd resign herself, and she'd acknowledge that Bilodo had the right to love whomever he pleased. It seemed to her that her life was drawing to a close, that all that was left was for her to die. In an earlier time, she would have entered a convent.

One night at the end of August, ill from having consumed too much pistachio ice cream, Tania decided that things couldn't continue as they were and resolved to go and see Bilodo. Not with the intention of winning him over – she forbade herself to harbour so much as an iota of hope on that subject – but in order to have a candid talk with him, to set the record straight, and to shed light on everything that had been festering in darkness since the unhappy tanka episode. Having done that, would she then be able to turn the page in complete serenity? Already dispossessed of everything, what did she have to lose?

Tania rang the doorbell. In her nervousness, she began to hope that Bilodo was out, but then, when she'd already turned on her heels, she heard the first in a series of metallic clicks. Several locks were unbolted. The door opened and Bilodo appeared. When she saw the way he looked, Tania froze. He hadn't shaved for months, and it had no doubt been just as long since a comb last touched the shaggy mane that fell to his shoulders. Bilodo had the complexion of a person buried alive, and dark circles surrounded his eyes. He was wearing a sort of red kimono. Tania felt as though she were standing before a stranger. The fresh, clean-shaven young postman, as straight as an arrow – where had he gone? How could he have transformed himself into this cave-dwelling hippie?

Bilodo's eyes were feverish. He looked exhausted. Tania, perplexed, asked him if he was all right, admitting that she found him quite changed. Bilodo smiled weakly – so it was him, after all – and averred that he'd never felt better in his life, although Tania remained unconvinced. He apologized confusedly for the tanka business, and for what had happened, but Tania assured him that she knew he was innocent. She attributed most of the blame to herself, she recognized that it had been her fault more than anyone else's, she proposed that it probably wouldn't have happened had she not let herself imagine... imagine certain things, isn't that right? Tania waited for Bilodo to confirm what she'd just said, or perhaps contradict it, but he didn't reply. Embarrassed, she changed the subject and informed him that she no longer worked at the Madelinot, and that she was going to move into a new apartment soon. She gave him her new address, in case he...if he should ever want...Bilodo examined the sheet of paper, on which she'd written her future contact details in Japanese-style calligraphy, with a brush.

'Give me a ring,' she ventured, 'if you feel like it.'
'Yes...'

An awkward moment followed. There they were, standing on the balcony, and Tania had a feeling that something was about to take place. It was one of those rare moments that come when you least expect them, and during which you feel that anything can happen, that the merest nothing would be enough to change your destiny for ever. Tania knew this was her time to speak, to make a gesture, but the fear of making a false step smothered her spontaneity, and all that she incredulously heard herself say was, 'Well, I have to go.' If Bilodo had reacted, if he'd asked her to stay, everything would still have been possible. But he remained silent.

The magic moment was over. Unwilling to burst into tears in front of him, Tania went down the steps. On the balcony, Bilodo seemed petrified. She swallowed her sobs and moved away, hoping he would implore her to come back. He did nothing of the sort. Tania quickened her pace, turned the corner into a little side street and it was only there, out of his sight, that she gave herself permission to liquefy.

On the pavement the wind was biting its own tail, making whirlwinds of newspaper scraps and dead leaves.

'Rue des Hêtres? Beech Street? Can somebody please tell me how it got that name? There's nothing here but bloody maples!' raged Tania, overcome by a mighty sense of injustice as she hurried along that absurd street, as absurd as her own existence. Had the street been planted with beeches in former times, and then those beeches replaced by maples? Or was the street's name the result of simple ignorance, the work of some old-time civil servant incapable of distinguishing between two different types of tree? 'Something must be done about this!' she exclaimed, getting excited. And suddenly she saw herself carrying that torch. The *Pasionaria* of arboricultural democracy, besieging the mayor's office, insisting that the street be renamed 'rue des Érables', Maple Street. Struggling to overcome the inertia of a resistant administration, canvassing the neighbourhood, raising citizen-awareness of the importance of this poetic issue. Gathering support, but nonetheless becoming the target of conservative factions opposed to changing a usage consecrated by centuries. Refusing to be intimidated, hoisting the banner of her cause all the higher, marching heroically at the head of her troops in tempestuous demonstrations that degenerated into riots, with fuel-doused maple trees set ablaze and chain-sawed beech trees crushing police vehicles, with signposts bearing the name of the accursed street torn down and brandished like halberds in an acrid fog of tear gas seasoned with cayenne pepper, and herself, Tania, attacked by a pro-beech extremist, hacked to death with a machete, elevated to martyr status, portrayed on T-shirts, and finally canonized...This strange sacrificial fantasy was obviously nothing more than a sophisticated form of mental escape that allowed her to channel her anger and her despair.

The sky was black, reflecting Tania's mood. A storm threatened. She went down into the subway and submitted to being hauled about by the train, with no more definite plan in mind than to get back home and inject herself with a fatal dose of pistachio ice cream.

Two stations further on, an octogenarian couple entered the carriage. Tania gave up her place so they could sit together. The fragile old lady placed her wrinkled hand in that of her companion. Moved at seeing them like that, still complicit in affection after so many years, Tania imagined herself in half a century, clinging to the arm of a solicitous Bilodo, still proud to be at her side. 'But that won't happen,' she told herself, mortified. Once again she evoked that special moment on the balcony, the one she'd been incapable of seizing. 'What were you waiting for, Tania Schumpf? Why didn't you try something?' In a delayed reaction, she thought about what she should have said, about what she could have done, and the analysis of her pathetic act of omission left her furious at herself. She resented her cowardice, the pusillanimous shyness that disabled her. Thus galvanized, she decided she wouldn't let things end like this. She would certainly not allow her beautiful love story to culiminate in so deplorable a failure. She left the subway carriage and boarded the train bound in the opposite direction, ready to go for broke and risk all.

'I'll tell him how much I love him,' she thought, conceiving a plan on the escalator that was carrying her back up to street level. 'And if words fail me, I'll kiss him: I'll make him see stars, and he'll know we're meant for each other.' When she emerged from the subway, Tania saw that the storm had burst. It was a veritable deluge, so heavy that for an instant it caused her to hesitate. But the fear that her resolution would crumble carried her on; resolved to act while she felt strong, Tania braved the elements.

She wasn't more than a hundred metres or so from Bilodo's building when she became aware that a crowd had gathered over there, right in front of his apartment. People were milling around a truck. An accident? Tania began to run, praying that her horrible premonition might not come true.

She broke through the circle of onlookers, ran around the truck, which had come to a stop in the middle of the street, moved closer...

Bilodo was lying on the wet asphalt. Just as in the nightmare that had frightened Tania after Gaston Grandpré's death. Except that this was no dream. It was appallingly real.

Robert was bending over Bilodo. When he saw Tania, he greeted her with a fatalistic gesture. She ignored him and knelt beside Bilodo. His beard was spattered with blood so thick that the rain, though torrential, failed to dilute it. His eyes were wide open, drowned by the downpour. His breathing had stopped.

'No!' cried Tania, protesting with all her might.

Because it was impossible. Bilodo couldn't do that to her. He had no right to die like that, at the moment when she was coming to offer him her heart; it was too cruel.

Robert tried to draw Tania away from what was now only a corpse. She pushed him away and began to give Bilodo mouth-to-mouth resuscitation. Robert maintained that it was useless, but she kept on nevertheless, deaf and blind to everything that wasn't Bilodo. She administered a cardiac massage and performed all the CPR manoeuvres she'd learned in the first-aid course she'd taken six years previously, never suspecting how crucially useful it would be to her one day.

When the ambulance came, Tania was still working away, keeping Bilodo artificially alive.

6

After a surgical intervention that lasted for six hours, Bilodo was transferred to Intensive Care, where Tania was allowed to see him. Finding him half-mummified in bandages and connected to an array of machines, she felt faint. Bilodo was unconscious. His beard had been shaved off, and so had his hair. His left leg was in a piteous state. A doctor explained to Tania that Bilodo's most severe injury, a skull fracture, had caused a major stroke. His fate remained uncertain: the next hours would be decisive. 'Fight, my love!' Tania urged Bilodo before she was obliged to leave the little room where he was hovering between life and death.

Tania spent an anxiety-ridden night in the hospital waiting room. She could still feel the chill on Bilodo's lips when she'd given him mouth-to-mouth resuscitation: far indeed from the first kiss she'd envisioned in her dreams. At the darkest point of that nocturnal vigil, she felt a moment of irrational panic upon seeing a black woman in the corridor – who turned out to be only a nurse. Tania reassured herself: Ségolène, at the other end of the galaxy, could know nothing of the drama that was being played out here; there was nothing to fear from that quarter, not in the short term, anyway. Besides, whatever the future might hold, Tania decided she'd acquired a right that the Guadeloupian woman could never claim: 'I saved Bilodo's life. He belongs to me from now on,' she told herself.

The following day, Bilodo was still breathing. The patient would survive, the doctor said, but he didn't dissemble the chances of serious after-effects caused by the oxygen deprivation Bilodo's brain had undergone during those too-long minutes when he was clinically dead. It was, for the moment, impossible to assess the extent of the said after-effects – they would have to perform tests once Bilodo regained consciousness. In the meantime, he'd been put into a medically induced coma to give his injured brain a better chance of healing. He would remain asleep in this way until his condition improved. The possibility of seeing Bilodo as a disabled person didn't frighten Tania. She felt ready to confront the worst ordeals. Having obtained permission to remain at Bilodo's bedside, she glued herself to a chair, resolved to watch over him for ever if necessary. 'I'm here, my love,' she murmured in Bilodo's unconscious ear, adjusting her heartbeats to the slow, hypnotic rhythm of the machine through which his heart was beeping.

The following afternoon, just when Tania was nodding off, a woman appeared in the room, carrying a bouquet of periwinkles. Tania, who knew nothing about Bilodo's family situation, presumed that this lady was some relative – his mother, perhaps? She introduced herself as Madame Brochu, declared herself to be Bilodo's landlady, the owner of the building in front of which the accident had occurred, and disclosed that she had witnessed, from her front porch, Tania's heroic intervention. 'What a calamity!' Madame Brochu exclaimed. 'If I had only known...If I could have foreseen...'

Tania pointed out that it had been an accident, unforeseeable by nature, but this observation was of scant comfort to Madame Brochu: 'I feel that it was to some extent my fault,' the lady said. 'I had nothing to do with it, needless to say, but I'm starting to wonder whether that apartment might not be jinxed. After all, this is the second tenant who's been hit by a truck in front of my house.'

'The second?' repeated Tania, surprised.

'Indeed,' Madame Brochu confirmed, looking guilty. 'A similar accident killed my previous tenant, poor Mr Grandpré.'

'Gaston Grandpré?' asked Tania in astonishment. 'You knew him?'

'Not really,' Tania stammered. 'He lived in your building?'

'Before Mr Bilodo, yes. A polite, respectful tenant – never a problem. That is, until the day when that truck ran over him right in front of the house, in exactly the same spot as Mr Bilodo, exactly a year later. It's weird, a coincidence like that, don't you think?'

45

Tania gazed at the sleeping Bilodo. Madame
Brochu's statement was correct: one year, to the day,
separated the two accidents. Tania thought back
to the feeling she'd had on the balcony when she
discovered Bilodo's astounding transformation, the
impression of his physical resemblance to someone
she hadn't been able to place right away, but whose
identity was now obvious – Gaston Grandpré. He
was the person Bilodo had put her in mind of.

Madame Brochu was right: so extraordinary a
coincidence couldn't be attributed to mere chance.
What could have impelled Bilodo to rent the
deceased's former apartment? And how to explain
the incredible repetition of the circumstances of
Grandpré's accident? What connection had there
been between the two men? Tania remembered that
Bilodo was greatly affected by Grandpré's death.
In the days following the passing of the man with
the red carnation, Bilodo had often come into the
restaurant and sat at the deceased's favourite table,
asking Tania to serve him what the late Grandpré
customarily ate and then chewing it morosely, his
nose to the window and a lost look in his eyes. Tania
had wondered why he was so troubled by the death
of a stranger. Grandpré had died in Bilodo's arms,
certainly a traumatizing experience, but Tania nevertheless found such a reaction excessive – as far as
she knew, the two men had never exchanged a single
word. Bilodo's lugubrious mood had fortunately
dissipated by the end of September, not long before

he'd been suddenly seized by a passion for Japanese poetry, and Tania had given no more thought to his previous gloom. But now she was compelled to admit that a relationship of some kind must have existed between Bilodo and Grandpré. But what could have been the nature of their secret bond?

'It's really too strange,' Madame Brochu went on. 'I'm afraid I have to inform the police.'

'The police?' Tania exclaimed. 'Why?'

Madame Brochu regarded her keenly and asked her to describe precisely what her connection to Bilodo was. Facing that piercing look without flinching, Tania asserted that she was a close friend.

'You appear to be a respectable girl,' Madame Brochu decided at last. 'I believe you have the right to know. Come,' she added, inviting Tania to accompany her.

'Come where?'

'To Mr Bilodo's. There's something I must show you.'

The key turned in the lock. Madame Brochu made it clear that she was not in the habit of letting herself into her tenants' quarters and that she had presumed to do so only as an exception after the ambulance workers had taken Bilodo away, because his door had remained open and she'd wanted to turn off that music – 'Chinese', she'd called it – that was still

47

playing in the empty apartment. As she stepped over the threshold of Bilodo's abode, Tania felt as though she'd been whisked away to the land of the rising sun. The furniture, the décor, the lamps – all were of Japanese inspiration or style. Wherever Tania's gaze rested, it encountered the tortured shape of a bonsai, a print, a statuette representing a languid geisha or a podgy bonze or a touchy samurai brandishing his sword. The floor was covered with tatami mats, soft carpets fitted together like pieces of a gigantic puzzle. Leading Tania into this exotic cave of wonders, Madame Brochu explained that Bilodo had turned up shortly after Grandpré's death and offered to rent the apartment. He'd insisted on taking it as it was, still furnished with the possessions of the deceased.

In a room that must have served as both a living and a dining room, embroidered cushions surrounded a low table on which lay a tiny Zen garden. There was also a fishbowl with a goldfish swimming in it. Tania supposed that this sea creature was none other than Bill, Bilodo's little aquatic companion, whose existence he'd revealed in a rare moment of confidence. Partitioned off by a screen painted with cherry trees in blossom, the second area of the room presumably served as a workspace: it contained a writing desk flanked by tall racks stuffed with books. And it was there that Madame Brochu, lifting a trembling finger, indicated the reason why she'd brought Tania to this spot: a cord hanging from a ceiling beam and ending in a slip knot.

The slip knot was gently swaying, even though there wasn't the slightest air current in the room, and Tania couldn't take her eyes off it. The cord must be the belt of a dressing gown – or rather of that kimono she'd seen Bilodo wearing on the balcony. The feverish look she'd seen in his eyes, the disillusioned expression on his face that she could at this point interpret only as that of a man who had given up on life...So he'd planned to hang himself. But he hadn't put his plan into action. Was it Tania's visit that had stopped him? Had he changed his mind after she left, choosing rather to imitate Grandpré by throwing himself under a truck? So many hypotheses, but one undeniable fact remained: Bilodo's injuries were due to a suicide attempt, not to an accident.

'What do you think about this?' Madame Brochu murmured. Averting her eyes from the visual attraction exercised by the slip knot, Tania turned towards the window. Rue des Hêtres stretched out in soft peace below her. Tania stared at the place in the middle of the road where she'd breathed back into Bilodo the life he had wanted to cut short. Whereas on the previous evening Tania had still been congratulating herself on having intervened in time, now she reproached herself for having been so late: had she arrived sooner, maybe she could have dissuaded Bilodo from committing such a senseless act. 'Just a little too late,' she thought regretfully. But then wasn't that the story of her peculiar relationship with Bilodo?

'I have to feed the fish. The poor little thing is starving,' said Madame Brochu.

While the lady was scattering yum-yums into the fishbowl where Bill had suddenly morphed into a piranha, Tania went over to the desk. Pinned on the wall above it was a photograph of a black woman. No doubt the famous Ségolène, for whose love Bilodo had become a poet. Tania was impressed by the Guadeloupian's beauty, by her beaming smile. Ségolène must be a teacher, for happy schoolgirls in uniform surrounded her in front of a blackboard, gazing at her with admiration that Tania found completely understandable, given the radiant aura of kind-heartedness that emanated from her. 'It's not surprising that Bilodo fell in love with her,' Tania sighed, finding herself desperately ordinary in comparison. How could the pallid Tania Schumpf compete with that charismatic islander?

The sheet of paper with Tania's future contact details lay on the desk. There was also Bilodo's mobile phone, along with various documents, but what magnetized Tania's attention were the haiku. Dozens of poems, carefully classified, forming a symmetrical stack. This must be Bilodo's poetic correspondence, she thought, the *renku* he was exchanging with Ségolène – and Tania felt the immediate conviction that this exchange held the key to the secret of Bilodo's tormented soul. The desire to know took possession of her. To satisfy her curiosity, to learn the reason why Bilodo had desired to kill himself, all she needed to do was to reach out her hand. However, not daring to make that move in Madame Brochu's presence, Tania pretended to feel only a superficial interest in the poems.

'We have to inform the authorities, don't you think?' asked the lady, staring at the slip knot with an anxious eye.

Tania wanted to avoid letting the police rummage through Bilodo's things, and so she recommended that Madame Brochu not tell anyone about the suicide attempt; she, Tania, promised to inform Bilodo's doctor about the matter herself, and he would know what measures to take in order to provide his patient with the appropriate psychological support. The lady greeted this solution with relief.

'I can also take care of feeding the fish,' Tania offered. 'I'll do some housekeeping at the same time.'

Madame Brochu accepted eagerly, pleased at not having to return any time soon to that apartment, which, she said, made her skin crawl. She gave a key to Tania, who saw her out. As soon as the lady was gone, Tania bolted the door and leaned back against it, satisfied: she now had free access to the place and could conduct her investigation as she wished. She would get to the heart of the mystery, and she'd discover what had plunged Bilodo into such distress that he had wanted to take his own life.

The first thing she did was to climb up on a chair and untie the cord that was hanging from the ceiling.

7

From the moss-cheeked volcano
dangles a chain of
slender waterfalls

A beach in HD
on a screen in the metro
sunshine guaranteed

Lofty royal palms
from their great height observing
a kid on his bike

Hard-charging caterpillar
running by itself
its own marathon

My neighbour Aimée
gardens in a floral dress
you would water her

The exchange continued like this, steadily, one poem per page. The haiku weren't dated, but knowing how meticulous Bilodo was, Tania supposed he'd kept them in chronological order.

Spicy, these accras!
they'd make a paralytic
dance a flamenco

Child takes her first steps
unknowing that at the end
her grave lies waiting

Two feathers and nothing else
in the open cage
the cat licks itself

The sleeping city
displays its belly
constellated gold and gems

Abracadabra!
the hat is empty
what's become of the rabbit?

Ségolène's haiku were scented with citrus oil and written in a pretty hand. Her poems alternated with Bilodo's, and each one acted in the manner of a dreamcatcher, trapping in the fine web of its seventeen syllables a fleeting vision, a flight of fancy, a shiny particle of eternity. They presented a bouquet of colourful images next to which Bilodo's everyday universe, the little prosaic world Tania was a part of, must have seemed pretty drab to him.

A Rorschach with blotted ink
saturates the sky
hurricane coming

These moving faces
images snatched from the wind
soon to disappear

Dancing to the beat
of the bola drums
she-devils of Carnival

Walking with head down
then I remember
the existence of the sky

Vanilla – curry
cinnamon – saffron
malangas – carambolas

After about fifty poems of the same crystalline kind, the form suddenly changed; Bilodo abandoned the haiku and came up with his first tanka. And Tania, who wasn't expecting it, found herself staring at the confession she'd had the weakness to believe was addressed to her:

Some flowers, it seems,
are seven years a-blooming
For a long time now

> I have longed to say to you
> all the love words in my heart

Tania was devastated at the sight of those lines. She regretted not having died the first time she'd read that poem, at the moment of her most perfect happiness; regretted having lived on, only to learn that she was but the caretaker of another's happiness; and especially regretted not being that other woman, whom Bilodo adored, but instead only Tania Schumpf, ordinary girl and mediocre poet. Burning nonetheless to know how Ségolène had responded to the postman's tender declaration, Tania turned the page. And what she read there took her breath away...The Guadeloupian had accompanied Bilodo to the land of feelings, but she hadn't settled for merely following his footsteps; she had most boldly taken the lead by sending him a resolutely aphrodisiac tanka:

> *Steamy, sultry night*
> *The moist sheets' soft embrace burns*
> *my thighs and my lips*
> *I search for you, lose my way*
> *I am that open flower*

These lines, obviously intended to titillate, had no doubt achieved their goal, for Bilodo, needing no further coaxing, had plunged headfirst into sensuality:

You are not just the flower
You're the whole garden
Your scents drive me wild
I enter your corolla
and I drink in your nectar

All petals outspread
I lean to you on my stem
From my tilted cup
drink the nectar I distil
drink to intoxication

Every drop of you I drink
only increases my thirst
I taste the honey
dripping from your lips
I revel unslaked in you

From then on, the poetry threw off all restraints,
turned breathless and panting, and the erotic tanka
verses were intermingled with some steamy haiku:

Your words have touched me
intimately caressed me
I'm still quivering

Think of all those words
you're quivering from
as so many single tongues

Denis Thériault

I cram my pillow
high and hard between my thighs
it isn't enough

Fortunate pillow
what joy to be in its place
clinched to your belly

I take you deep inside me
I'm utterly filled with you
Your heat plus my heat equals
temperature close to
liquefaction point

Your breath's growing short
I'm groaning into your ear
and sighing your name

Suddenly in spate
the raging river
overflowing my delta

I fall in all directions
hanging on to you
everywhere at once

From our own Big Bang
a new universe is born
of endless pleasures

She was getting hot, Tania noticed, and all of a sudden she felt ashamed of herself, feeding like a vampire on other people's emotions. To calm her excited senses, she took a shower, gradually decreasing the proportion of hot water. Shortly afterwards, having cooled off and prepared a cup of strong coffee, she judged herself fit to go on. Once again, she sat down with the poems in front of her. They continued for a few more pages to rise towards a kind of erotic-poetic climax, but then the tone changed: the tanka genre returned in force, and the poems became tender, like so many sweet secrets whispered in a lover's ear.

> *I dream about waking up*
> *from sleep by your side*
> *into a bright dawn*
> *surely the most beautiful*
> *of all mornings in the world*

> I hate the geography
> that keeps us apart
> but what does distance matter
> on the map of my heart there's
> nothing separating us

> *I'm inventing us*
> *our own private world*
> *where time no longer exists*
> *an eternal Saturday*
> *an unending fifth season*

Bilodo and Ségolène exchanged a few more of these horribly romantic poems, and then the chain ended with a tanka from the Guadeloupian woman, five lines that seemed to constitute the most recent dispatch:

> *As a child I dreamt*
> *of Canada's bright autumn*
> *I have bought my ticket I*
> *arrive on the twentieth*
> *Will you have me, then?*

This could mean only one thing: Ségolène was announcing her arrival in Montreal on the twentieth of September – that is, in a little more than two weeks. Tania felt her stress level skyrocketing. The Guadeloupian's approaching visit would surely reduce to nil Tania's already slim chance of conquering Bilodo. Would she not be instantaneously eclipsed by a Ségolène in flesh and blood, who needed only to appear in all her glorious beauty for Bilodo to swoon and cast himself at her feet?

Tania had the nightmarish sensation that the walls were closing in around her.

Bilodo had been transferred to a room where he was being kept under observation. He slept, connected to the world only by the network of wires and tubes that probed him and nourished him. Soothed by the hushed atmosphere of the room, Tania relaxed a little. Her critical faculties seized the opportunity to take over, and a sudden question dawned on her: was there some connection between Ségolène's impending arrival and Bilodo's suicide attempt?

Logically speaking, the imminent prospect of a face-to-face meeting with the woman he'd been loving from afar should have enthralled Bilodo. But to all appearances, the prospect had instead prompted him to take his own life. How to explain this emotional incoherence? Why had the announcement of Ségolène's visit produced such a devastating effect on Bilodo?

Out of her depth, Tania had to settle for chalking up this new mystery on her mental slate. After conducting an initial inventory of the elements she'd been able to gather in her investigation, she had to acknowledge that the results were pretty slim. The nature of the relationship linking Bilodo to Grandpré remained opaque, and the similarity between their two accidents was still incomprehensible. What was it about, all that?

Ségolène would arrive in two weeks' time, which meant that Tania had no more than a fortnight to clear up this multi-faceted mystery, and then to decide on a course of action.

Tania examined the desk drawers. The first one contained calligraphy materials, various articles related to the art of haiku and Gaston Grandpré's death notice.

The second drawer was filled with personal papers, a birth certificate, and other documents attesting to Bilodo's official existence. In an envelope, Tania found a newspaper clipping, a report on an accident that had taken place in Vieux-Québec, the oldest part of Québec City, four years previously. She remembered the accident, for it had made a great stir: the cables of a funicular had broken, and the cable car had crashed to the foot of the bluff, causing seven deaths. Two documents and a photograph accompanied the article. The documents were the death certificates of Alain Bilodo, 53, and Nancy Lavoie-Bilodo, 49, two names that, as Tania observed, also appeared on the list of the accident victims. The photograph, which was older and had apparently been taken a number of years before the tragedy, pictured three members of a family, posing in front of what Tania guessed was the funicular in question: a man and a woman with depressed faces stood on either side of a skinny little boy whom Tania recognized to be Bilodo at perhaps ten years of age. Wedged between the two adults, little Bilodo looked vaguely terrorized. Tania was moved when she read the inscription on the back of the photo: 'Maman, Papa, and me in Vieux-Québec.' Bilodo's handwriting intrigued her; it wasn't the same as the one he used when composing his haiku. Trying to explain the dissimilarity, Tania assumed that the words before her had been written a long time ago, in a child's hand.

The third drawer was locked. Tania searched the apartment for the key. In the process, she made some unusual discoveries, such as the dried-flower collection – Grandpré's, in all likelihood – in which a red carnation dried long ago was glued to each page; there was also, in the chest of drawers in the bedroom, an amazing assortment of unmatched socks, hundreds of them, enough to make a giant millipede happy. At last, rifling through the pockets of Bilodo's postman's jacket, Tania fished out a bunch of keys, one of which fitted in the lock on the third drawer.

It turned out to be a filing cabinet, in which several file folders were hanging. The first ones contained hundreds of photocopies of personal letters, obviously penned by as many different hands. The oldest of these letters dated back four years, and they came from more or less everywhere, from as far away as Port-Cartier, Whitehorse, Salem, Las Vegas, Kandahar, Melbourne...None of them, however, was addressed to Bilodo, and Tania, puzzled, wondered how he'd been able to assemble such a collection of private writings. Was it possible that...

It seemed incredible, but could it be that Bilodo was an inquisitive postman, one who secretly read and copied certain letters before delivering them?

It wasn't so implausible when you were familiar with Bilodo's peculiar character. Tania had a mental image of him making his daily round and finding in his bag a personal letter, a thing that has become rare in this highly connected age of electronic messaging. Actually, it was easy to imagine Bilodo intercepting two or three letters a week like that, taking them home, steaming them open, and making copies of them before delivering them to their true addressees the next day. It was only a hypothesis, but Tania had no difficulty conceiving it: a complete loner like Bilodo just might take great pleasure in infiltrating other people's lives that way.

Passing from surprise to surprise, Tania pulled from the next folder a manuscript titled *Enso*, whose cover page had an illustration of a black circle with a frayed outline – and whose author was none other than Gaston Grandpré. Intrigued, she opened the manuscript and looked at the first page, on which were printed only three lines:

> Swirling like water
> against rugged rocks,
> time goes around and around

The manuscript numbered about sixty pages, on each of which appeared a different haiku. Grandpré too, she concluded, had gone in for Japanese poetry, and seriously enough to have produced a collection of poems.

Enclosed with the manuscript was an unsealed letter, in which Bilodo authorized Éditions Fibonacci to publish the manuscript *Enso*. Bilodo, it seemed, had taken the posthumous initiative of submitting Grandpré's collection to the Montreal-based publishing house, which had accepted it. Tania noted that the date on the unsigned letter corresponded to the very day of Bilodo's suicide attempt: he'd neglected to post the letter before trying to end his life.

Putting the manuscript aside, Tania examined the contents of the last folder, which proved disappointing: fifty or so open, empty envelopes, each bearing Guadeloupian stamps and each with Ségolène's address in Pointe-à-Pitre in the upper left-hand corner. An inspection of the postmarks revealed that the envelopes had been sent during the course of the preceding twelve months – and had no doubt contained the Guadeloupian woman's haiku. Tania sighed. She now had reason to believe that Bilodo was a sort of postal voyeur, and Grandpré's manuscript established a direct link between the two men. Her investigation was making progress, and yet she couldn't get rid of the irritating impression that she was getting nowhere. 'What a sorry detective you make, Tania Schumpf!' she said to herself as she put the empty envelopes back into their folder. It was then that a detail leaped out at her: the envelopes were addressed to Grandpré.

Not to Bilodo, but to Gaston Grandpré.

Tania systematically verified this observation; they were addressed to the deceased, every one of them. For a brief, cloudy moment, she understood nothing. So Grandpré was the person Ségolène was writing to? Or believed she was writing to? Then something clicked, and she saw that the haiku must originally have been meant for Grandpré. Not knowing he'd been dead for more than a year, the Guadeloupian had continued to write to him, without suspecting that it was Bilodo who was reading her letters and replying to her.

This was the only explanation that could fully account for the facts: Bilodo had taken Grandpré's place.

It must have been while acting as the inquisitive postman that Bilodo had become aware of Grandpré and Ségolène's poetic correspondence and fallen madly in love with the beautiful Guadeloupian. When Grandpré's death had threatened to dry up the source of that cherished correspondence, Bilodo had made the audacious decision to take the lately departed's place. His calligraphic talent had enabled him to imitate Grandpré's handwriting without too much difficulty, but even so, he'd still had to learn the basics of Japanese poetry; Tania remembered his sudden enthusiasm for the art of haiku.

Following that strange logic of substitution to its extreme, Bilodo had rented the dead man's apartment and moved in, receiving there the poems intended for Grandpré and responding to them in his stead – and all for the love of Ségolène.

Such, therefore, was the nature of the obsession that was consuming Bilodo. And this also explained the proximate cause of his suicide attempt: the arrival of the poem in which Ségolène announced she was coming to Montreal. Bilodo had realized that he was trapped, for the Guadeloupian woman and Grandpré had exchanged photographs, and she knew what he looked like – and thus Bilodo's imaginary world had collapsed. The mental process that had led to his identification with the deceased, an identification so complete that he'd recreated the circumstances of the other's death, remained obscure, but his reason for doing so was now obvious: it was his certainty that he would soon be unmasked. Rather than reveal to Ségolène that he was an impostor, Bilodo had preferred to kill himself.

The doctor informed Tania that the blood in Bilodo's brain resulting from his stroke was being satisfactorily reabsorbed. If his condition continued to improve, his sedation dosage could be decreased, and he could be gradually brought out of his artificial coma. 'Don't worry,' the doctor said. 'He'll wake up eventually.'

'But in what state of mind?' Tania wondered, studying Bilodo's lethargic features.

Because he was, without any doubt, daft.

To act the way he'd done, Bilodo simply had to have gone mad. But what right did Tania have to condemn his actions? Had she shown herself lately to be so much more rational than he was? Didn't her own recent actions demonstrate that she was as daft as Bilodo, and that they were therefore perfectly matched?

'Yes, Tania Schumpf,' she scolded herself, 'you're mad to love such a madman!' Her reason told her to flee before she lost the plot altogether, to run away and not come back. But instead she leaned over Bilodo and planted a tender kiss on his lips. She wanted to see him wake up smiling, as in the fairytales, but his eyelids remained sealed. He lay before her, vulnerable, and Tania's duty manifested itself to her with dazzling clarity. She knew her role was to protect Bilodo. Protect him from himself, from the whims that disoriented him, but first and foremost from the diabolical Guadeloupian woman who would soon be deplaning in Montreal.

The woman must not get anywhere near Bilodo. He'd never wanted her to come, he'd feared her coming so much that he'd preferred to throw himself under a truck. In his extremely weakened state, the consequences of such a confrontation could be nothing short of dramatic – it might even provoke another suicide attempt. And that was something Tania would not permit. She would do everything she could to prevent any meeting from taking place.

'Fear not, my love,' she whispered in Bilodo's ear. 'I won't let that woman do you any harm.'

9

Unless Ségolène's aeroplane conveniently vanished into thin air over the Bermuda Triangle, she'd arrive on the twentieth. And then what would happen?

She would wait at the airport for her dear pen pal Grandpré. Who would present himself, if at all, only in spectral form. The Guadeloupian would probably take a cab to the apartment on rue des Hêtres, whose address she knew, and where she would come up against a definitively closed door. Could it be hoped that such inhospitality would suffice to discourage her and prompt her to return to her island on the next flight? Too good to be true. Ségolène wouldn't give up so easily. She'd knock on the neighbours' doors, ask questions, and inevitably end up face-to-face with Madame Brochu, who would inform her that Gaston Grandpré had been dead for more than a year. As soon as she recovered from the initial shock, Ségolène would attempt to learn her correspondent's real identity; she'd grill Madame Brochu, who wouldn't fail to steer her towards Bilodo. Could Tania obtain Madame Brochu's cooperation? Or was there any way to make sure the old lady wasn't home when Ségolène turned up? In any case, Grandpré's unexplained absence would surely alarm Ségolène, who would eventually report his disappearance to the police.

How to erase the trail leading to Bilodo? Or how to cover it so well that Ségolène wouldn't be able to follow it all the way to him?

Dear Madame Ségolène,

I am writing to let you know that you are the victim of a hoax. It is my painful duty to inform you that your correspondent Gaston Grandpré died last year. The poems you have continued to receive are the work of an impostor who has written to you since Mr Grandpré's death, passing himself off as the deceased, with disastrous consequences for his own mental health: upon learning of your impending visit, he tried to kill himself. He is currently in hospital, in a serious condition. For your own sake, but also for his, I implore you to cancel your journey and put an end to your correspondence. Stay where you are, and don't write to him any more. Thank you for your understanding.

From someone who wishes you well.

Tania put down her pen and reread her letter. She wasn't satisfied with it. When Ségolène learned she'd been deceived, she would probably cancel her trip and set about dynamiting all the bridges connecting her with the impostor; however, posting that letter didn't guarantee a definitive resolution of the problem. Disastrous consequences could ensue. The Guadeloupian might take offence and demand an apology, or maybe even some kind of reparation for emotional injury. Or she might have a contrary reaction, and the sad fate of the author of those marvellous haiku could move her enough to overcome her indignation and rush to his bedside on the next flight. Not to mention all the other forms that catastrophe might possibly take.

Upon reflection, Tania concluded that it would be best not to post the letter – the effects it might cause were too unpredictable. She was back at square one, and the question, reformulated, presented itself in these terms: how to push the Guadeloupian woman away from Bilodo without revealing the truth to him? Buried in thought, Tania jumped at a sudden, loud clack that came from the cover of the letterbox in the front door – the postman had just passed. She went to see, absent-mindedly, and froze on the threshold of the doorway. On the floor, waiting for her, was a letter from Ségolène.

Will you have me, then?
 Your silence troubles my heart
Answer me quickly

Tania reread this haiku for the umpteenth time, doing her best to grasp all of its implications. 'Bilodo hasn't answered her last poem,' she deduced. And in fact, that was obvious; why would he have responded? What could he have replied to the announcement of a visit that left him no way out except death?

Ségolène had guessed something was awry; the tone of her haiku proved that. Having waited in vain for a reply from Grandpré, she was beginning to doubt, and she wanted to confirm that she would be welcome in Montreal. Which changed the situation completely. 'She won't dare come without an invitation,' Tania realized, with immense relief. The problem would resolve itself, and suddenly she felt as if she was floating. She gave outward expression to her joy, skipping around like a little girl, dancing in the middle of the living room, planting a kiss on Bill's fishbowl: 'Sé-go-lè-ne won't be com-ing...' she sang to the wriggling fish, which was as excited as she was.

After a while, she restrained herself. 'Don't gloat too soon, Tania Schumpf, the game isn't over yet,' her inner voice warned her, forcing her feet back down to earth, because the most delicate challenge of all still lay before her. Ségolène probably wouldn't come, and thus a major obstacle would be removed, but Bilodo wasn't going to forget her so easily: she, Tania, must lead him to recognize that the beautiful Guadeloupian had been but a mirage, and that she, Tania, was the only real woman in his life.

On the twentieth of September, Tania anxiously watched dawn break over the city. The sole flight from Guadeloupe that day was scheduled to land at one forty-five in the afternoon. Would the Guadeloupian dare? Unable to confirm Ségolène's presence on the passenger list – confidential information – Tania crossed rue des Hêtres at two o'clock and sat on the terrace of a café that directly faced the apartment. It was an ideal lookout post; there was no possibility of her missing Ségolène's arrival, if she should come.

Tania waited. The hours passed. Ségolène wasn't coming. The watchful Tania waited some more... Finally, at eight in the evening, calculating that an appearance on the part of the Guadeloupian was no longer to be feared, Tania allowed herself to leave her observation post. Apparently, Ségolène had understood that her presence was undesirable – and Tania felt almost grateful to her.

Tania confidently crossed the street again and rang Madame Brochu's doorbell. Saying that she was there on Bilodo's behalf, Tania gave the lady a notice of non-renewal of his lease on the apartment. Madame Brochu was disappointed to see her quiet, trouble-free tenant go. Tania promised that the apartment would be completely vacated by the end date on the lease (in late October) and then she went up to Bilodo's and fed Bill. The apartment contained little in the way of heavy furniture, but she would nevertheless need to hire some movers and put everything in storage. Tania turned on the computer and did a little Internet research, trying to compile a list of moving companies she could contact. A few notes of Japanese music signalled an incoming email. Curious, Tania performed the appropriate clicks. It was a message from Ségolène:

> Aeroplane takes flight
> carries off the fall
> I'd dreamt of for you and me

'You can always dream!' thought Tania, refusing to let herself be moved by the distress emanating from the haiku. Just in case, she made a note of Ségolène's email address, and then, with a merciless click, she added her name to the list of blocked senders, and with another one deleted her message. If the Guadeloupian woman had only a little common sense, she wouldn't be heard from again.

Over the course of the following days, there was – except in Tania's nightmares – no sign of Ségolène. Tania dismissed that particular worry from her immediate preoccupations and devoted herself to Bilodo, assiduously watching over him. The hospital staff stopped giving him the sedatives that were keeping him unconscious, and Tania was assured that he'd wake up naturally, some day soon. Caring for Bilodo occupied all her attention; this was not the moment to be moving house, and so Tania cancelled the lease on the suburban apartment where she'd planned to transfer her home. Instead she once again rented her present place, for which, luckily, a new tenant had not yet been found.

Weary as she was, Tania almost failed to hear her telephone ringing a little before midnight on the second of October. It was a nurse from the Intensive Care unit, informing her that Bilodo had opened his eyes.

'Amnesia?' said Tania in dismay.

'I'm afraid so,' the doctor replied. He'd insisted on speaking with her in private before letting her see Bilodo. 'That was one of the possible consequences I told you about, a result of the head trauma he suffered.'

'He remembers nothing at all?'

'He can recall his youth, but later memories get vaguer and vaguer. The last six years of his life are a black hole.'

'So he's lost his memory for ever?' Tania asked worriedly.

'That's impossible to say. His amnesia might perhaps be only temporary, but it could also be permanent. We'll learn more over the course of the next few days.'

Tania was granted permission to see Bilodo but cautioned against tiring him. Stopping on the threshold of his room, she glanced inside furtively. Bilodo was staring wild-eyed at the ceiling. Some of his bandages had been removed. An ugly scar adorned his shaved skull. He looked like a zombie.

'Hello,' said Tania, venturing into the room.

Bilodo turned a concave stare on her. 'Who are you?' he asked in a broken voice.

Tania hid her consternation. The doctor hadn't been exaggerating: Bilodo seemed to have no memory of her.

'I'm Tania,' she replied simply.

'Tania?' Bilodo croaked, examining her distraughtly. 'Tania...' he repeated, making a laborious effort to process the information. 'Do we know each other?'

Tania opened her mouth, on the point of reminding him who she was and how she'd saved his life... but no word passed her lips. She kept silent, suddenly aware of the potential implications of the situation: if Bilodo didn't remember her, the odds were excellent that he'd forgotten Ségolène as well.

Then an idea germinated inside Tania. It was a frighteningly bold idea, at once brilliant and demented, which proliferated at lightning speed and ignited the fires of her imagination; it was the opportunity she'd long been waiting for, the perfect solution to her quandary. Seizing her chance, she replied to Bilodo: 'Of course we know each other. I'm your fiancée.'

10

Bilodo needed to be told what year it was. He had no recollection whatsoever of his near-fatal accident. When Tania described how she had kept him alive until help came, he expressed his profound gratitude. Although surprised to find himself equipped with a fiancée, he hadn't disputed the notion and in fact seemed to accept it, even though it caused him a certain embarrassment. What troubled him most was the unfathomable void into which the most recent years of his life had fallen. Bilodo remembered that he was a postman, but he'd forgotten that he worked and lived in the Saint-Janvier-des-Âmes district. Questioning him warily, Tania determined that he conserved no memory of the Madelinot or of the Depot. He recalled the old neighbourhood where he'd once lived and delivered the post, but nothing after that; it had all been erased. While examining Bilodo's personal documents, Tania discovered that this snip in his temporal thread corresponded to the time six years previously when Canada Post had transferred him to Saint-Janvier, a reassignment that had surely represented a major change for him: new environment...new postal route...new existence...It was no accident that the caesura in his memory was placed at just that moment of great upheaval.

The first living creature Bilodo asked about was

81

Bill, his goldfish, who'd been sharing his world long enough to pre-date the forgotten years. Tania assured him that his little finny friend was doing fine. Checking Bilodo's current status with the Post, she was able to confirm that everything was in order; he was on official sick leave for a period of time to be determined by the doctor treating him, who decreed that Bilodo's convalescence would require six months.

Eager to learn more about himself, Bilodo bombarded Tania with questions. She answered them as thoroughly as she could, taking care to avoid saying anything that might remind him of Ségolène or Grandpré. She had worked out appropriate responses to all the queries she thought Bilodo likely to come up with. Having painstakingly accumulated every scrap of information about him she could find, she believed she was in a position to provide him with any biographical detail that ought to be known by a fiancée genuinely worthy of the name.

Too preoccupied with his memory problems, or maybe too bashful, Bilodo had at first skirted the delicate subject of their romantic relationship. It wasn't until the second day after his awakening that he dared to inquire about what had gone on between them: 'How did we...meet?' he stammered.

'Here we go,' Tania thought, having waited

apprehensively for this sensitive topic to come up. As part of her meticulous preparation, she'd invented a mutual past for them, tailor-made and woven out of tender remembrances. 'I hope I haven't left anything out,' she thought, nervous – now that the moment had come – about submitting her fable to Bilodo. Mixing certain elements of reality into her fiction to give it more verisimilitude, Tania told him they'd met during the previous winter, in a restaurant where she worked as a waitress, and they'd liked each other at first sight. As Bilodo was greedy for details, Tania described their first exchanges, all ogling and smiling, discreet harbingers of their ensuing courtship, which had soon become urgent on both sides. One morning, arriving to open the restaurant, Tania had found a mysterious package in front of the door, and in it a single red rose, romantically wrapped in black silk paper. A charming gesture, to which she'd responded later that same day, after Bilodo had finished his lunch, by drawing an arrow-pierced heart on his bill. The following morning, a florist had come to the restaurant and buried Tania under twelve dozen roses. Not long after noon, Bilodo was served a cottage pie lovingly cut into the shape of a heart. He'd invited Tania to go out with him. She'd suggested ice-skating, and one January evening, in the middle of the frozen pond in Bonsecours Basin Park, they'd kissed for the first time.

'I see,' said Bilodo, flabbergasted.

'We quickly became inseparable. We used to say

we couldn't live without each other,' declared Tania, lying with a self-assurance that impressed even her, and which she justified by persuading herself that it was only a question of slightly dressing up the truth in order to repair a sort of technical error.

For that was the way she saw the matter: a case of confusion on the part of Destiny. In Tania's eyes, she and Bilodo had been fated to meet and fall in love, and their botched romantic union stemmed from a karmic dysfunction which she felt it her legitimate right to remedy. She would force the future, whose course had inadvertently shifted, back into its natural channel, and thus she would restore the proper order of the universe. Her plan was perfectly laid out. She would erase all trace of Ségolène and Grandpré from Bilodo's past. She'd burn all the haiku. She'd buy Bilodo a new telephone, whose number she alone would know. Later, when he was released from the hospital, she'd take him to live with her in her home by making him believe it was 'their place'. Then all that would remain for her to do would be to cultivate Bilodo's feelings so adroitly that in the end he would fall into her arms, and the initial lie would be transformed into a glorious truth. Such was Tania's project.

The next day, Bilodo was joyfully surprised when Tania placed on his bedside table a fishbowl in which his goldfish was swimming about blithely. 'Bill!' exclaimed the delighted Bilodo.

'I thought you'd be happy to see him,' said Tania, glad to afford him this pleasure.

She'd decanted Bill into a bowl equipped with a lid and come to the hospital in a taxi in order to maximize the fish's comfort. She would have to take him with her when she left, for the rules strictly prohibited the introduction of companion animals into the patients' rooms; nevertheless, Tania was proud of having been able to obtain this special permission by negotiating with the nursing staff.

Seeming to recognize Bilodo, who was leaning over his bowl, Bill shuddered and started going round in frenetic circles. 'I think he missed you,' Tania said, offering her interpretation of the fish's natatorial language.

'So do I,' Bilodo declared. 'I can't wait to recover. I want my memory back, most of all.'

'There's no reason to rush things. First you have to take enough time to get really well,' Tania hastened to reply. She had some very different priorities.

Bilodo didn't think of letting his parents know what had happened to him until two days later. Because he had no relatives better qualified to carry out the lugubrious task, Tania took it upon herself to inform him that his progenitors were no longer of this world, having been the victims of a funicular accident – a piece of news to which Bilodo reacted with remarkable composure. Tania inferred from this that his familial relations must never have been very warm-hearted.

'I remember that funicular,' Bilodo confided. 'I was scared of it when I was little. After our Sunday stroll through the Basse-Ville, my parents loved to take the cable car back up, but I refused to get in. I'd take the stairs and wait for them at the top, on the Terrasse Dufferin. I loved those stairs. I'd count them. There were two hundred and twenty-six...'

Tania liked to imagine little Bilodo light-footedly climbing the steps in Vieux-Québec while counting them aloud. Then another image imposed itself on her mind: the adult Bilodo, now a postman, bounding athletically up the exterior staircases along rue des Hêtres, counting the stairs in a low voice. At the Madelinot, his colleagues showed that they were quite familiar with this idiosyncrasy: 'How many steps this morning, Bilodo?' they'd call out to him as soon as he walked through the door. 'One thousand four hundred and fifteen,' he would reply, without hesitation. And the postal workers would burst into guffaws, considering this odd habit just another sign of Bilodo's eccentricity. They didn't know that what looked to them like an absurd quirk had its origin in obscure childhood dread, in a child's prescient fear of a terrifying machine and the fatal premonition it inspired in him.

'Montmartre!' Tania said, falling into a dream. Paris and Montmartre and its famous stairs, so romantic: that's where she would take Bilodo one day. Yes, Montmartre to start with, because that would be only the beginning; the world abounded in stairs just waiting to be taken by a couple of true lovers. 'When your legs get strong again, we'll climb the stairs of a new life together, and I'll count every step with you,' she promised Bilodo silently.

11

An MRI scan revealed a benign lesion on Bilodo's prefrontal cortex. However, the neurologist doubted that this lesion was the cause of Bilodo's amnesia, and a psychiatrist was called in as a back-up. A short woman of ineffable age, Justine Tao had minuscule dreamcatchers adorned with pink feathers dangling from her ears; she seemed incapable of harming a fly without having first analysed it. Tania, not authorized to be present at Dr Tao's interview with Bilodo, went to the waiting room, where she sat biting her nails and dreading the shrink's conclusions. Justine Tao joined her there an hour later, and she confirmed what Tania had hoped: Bilodo's memory remained sequestered. Tao suspected the activation of a psychological defence mechanism by which Bilodo could unconsciously avoid remembering some unbearably traumatic event. 'Had he seemed stressed of late?' she asked. 'Any abnormal behaviour?'

'Apart from reading other people's post, falling in love with a total stranger, taking a dead man's place and throwing himself under a truck, you mean?' Tania was tempted to reply sarcastically. But she contented herself with asserting that she hadn't noticed anything in particular.

'You and he are engaged, isn't that so? This amnesia must be an awful experience for you,' Tao said sympathetically. 'You must feel terribly helpless...'

Treading carefully, Tania acknowledged that it was indeed difficult, but she was bearing up. Tao assured her that she could play an active role in unlocking Bilodo's memory and recommended that Tania put him in contact with what his existence had been over the course of recent years: 'As soon as he's sufficiently recovered, have him meet people he knows, his old friends. Take him to the places he used to frequent, remind him of what his habits were. And be on the lookout for possible *flashbacks*,' she concluded, using the English word.

'*Flashbacks*?' asked Tania, puzzled.

'Bits of memory that arise unexpectedly, out of the blue. Were they to appear in Bilodo's case, they would be an indication that things were starting to come back to him. And the best way to provoke flashbacks is to stimulate his senses.'

'His senses?'

'Sensory memory is an excellent psychological trigger. Have Bilodo taste flavours you know he likes, have him listen to things and smell things. Sometimes all it takes is a familiar sound or smell, and then something clicks. If Bilodo ever has a flashback, encourage him to untangle the images and explore the memory.'

Tania promised to follow these recommendations, but refrained from saying that she'd do so in reverse. The shrink's advice actually seemed quite useful to Tania, as long as she did exactly the opposite: she would strive to remove from Bilodo's environment anything at all that risked evoking his past.

Ignorant of what his 'fiancée' was plotting, Bilodo asked her, as soon as she went back to his room, to describe to him again the way they were before his accident. Tania complied with this request by shamelessly filching inspiration from certain touching scenes in her favourite romantic comedies and portraying the two of them bathed in heavenly light, a pair of blissful lovebirds. Bilodo took all this in without discussion – as far as Tania could tell, he believed it.

'I see,' he said, even though his blindness was evident. 'And when did we plan to get married?'

'We hadn't fixed a definite date yet,' Tania ventured. 'In any case, we have to wait until you're well.'

'Of course. Let's wait a bit,' Bilodo agreed, looking pensive.

'What were you on, some kind of drug cocktail?' Noémie exclaimed.

'You're the one who wanted me to do something. I followed your advice.'

'All right, fine, but this is insane. And it will never work.'

'Oh yes it will, it's going to work!' Tania replied, a little regretful for having confided in her friend.

'Bilodo's not questioning our engagement. He's getting used to the idea.'

'The idea won't ever go the distance. He'll end up finding out the truth,' Noémie prophesized.

'There is a risk,' Tania admitted, 'but it's very small. He has no parents and no relatives who could undeceive him or give me away.'

'What about the Guadeloupian woman? What will you do if she won't let go?'

'If she's stupid enough to show up here, I'll sort her out,' Tania said trenchantly.

'Have you gone completely nuts?' Noémie replied, amazed at this hitherto unseen, fearsome Tania. 'Your Bilodo isn't some computer hard disk you can simply reformat the way you want. Even if you manage to reprogram his emotions, what will you do the day his memory returns?'

'That will probably never happen,' Tania maintained stubbornly.

'Rubbish! Sooner or later, he'll remember. For sure!'

Tania took refuge in silence, unable to deny the existence of an uncomfortably uncertain factor. That was the weak point in her plan, and she knew it. How long would Bilodo remain an amnesiac? What would she do if he recovered his memory? What could she say in her defence, except that she'd believed she was acting for his own good?

When she entered Bilodo's room, she found him watching television: a documentary about the South Pole and penguin migration.

He was crying.

When he saw Tania, Bilodo removed his earphones and tried his best to suppress his sobs.

'Why are you crying?' she dared to whisper.

'I can't remember,' Bilodo said desolately.

'That's normal. The doctor said it would take time.'

'I can't remember us, I can't remember our love. I'm sorry,' he said, sounding lost.

'It's not your fault...'

'I feel empty. I'm afraid I don't know how to love you any more,' Bilodo said in despair.

Pained to see him in such distress, Tania wondered whether Noémie might not be right about her: hadn't she gone too far in so inconsiderately proclaiming herself to be Bilodo's fiancée? Wasn't she wrong to interfere with his mind that way, and by so doing wasn't she committing some kind of mental rape?

Nevertheless, Bilodo seized her hands and pressed them between his. 'I don't remember loving you,' he said, 'but I understand very well why I did: you're adorable, Tania.'

'No,' she protested. That compliment, which in other circumstances would have propelled her into the seventh heaven, sounded bitter now.

'Let's start again,' Bilodo proposed. 'I don't know if I'll be able to love you as well as before, but I'm going to try. Will you help me?'

'Of course,' replied Tania in an irresolute voice.

'I know I can count on you.'

Tania found the strength to smile, but only in order to hide her shame at being so undeserving of Bilodo's trust. 'It's now or never, Tania Schumpf!' her little inner voice said. 'If you must set the record straight, now's the time to do it, before you cause any more damage.' And Tania knew that this was indeed the moment. After all, there was nothing obliging her to mention Ségolène. She'd limit herself to confessing that she'd exaggerated a little in telling the story of their engagement, that she'd let herself get carried away by her feelings. It was no doubt better for Bilodo to learn the truth from her lips, while he still had no memory of the Guadeloupian woman, rather than from some other, uncontrollable source when Tania least expected it.

'Bilodo, I'm not the perfect girl you think I am,' she began.

'I love you,' Bilodo solemnly declared.

His voice was firm, his eyes candid. He wanted what he'd said to be true, he was doing everything he could to convince himself it was. Tania's throat tightened. Incapable of continuing her confession, she fell silent, terribly aware that her silence was tantamount to passing a point of no return, beyond which honesty would no longer be possible. From now on, Tania would have no other choice but to make that enormous lie work, to go all the way. Needless to say, sooner or later Bilodo would have to learn the truth. On some future day, when time had given their love solid enough roots, when she felt that Bilodo was strong enough to understand and forgive, on that day, yes, Tania would speak. But not now, when everything was still hanging by a thread, and when the slightest false move could precipitate them into the abyss. Not today.

On the television, two penguins were pressing themselves together, surrounded by frozen infinitude, sheltering each other from the cold Antarctic wind.

12

They didn't go out very often. Sometimes they went to the cinema, the restaurant, or the health spa, but they preferred to remain in their apartment and surrender themselves to the tranquil stay-at-home pleasures of 'cocooning': thus Tania presented their former manner of life to Bilodo, who was always eager to learn more about the way they were. She took advantage of his curiosity to give him a detailed description of 'their' apartment. Casually, as though in passing, Tania was preparing Bilodo to move in with her.

A nurse came to deliver Bilodo's meal. Tania turned on an electric candle for a bit of ambience. She set her mobile phone to play some music and then unwrapped the Greek salad she'd brought from the Petit Malin. She had taken up the pleasant habit of eating with Bilodo when she visited him after work.

'I'm not hungry,' Bilodo declared, considering the contents of his tray with a mistrustful eye.

Tania understood his reluctance: on the plate lay two slices of a mysterious meat, and beside them were a pathetic islet of purée and a few limp green beans.

Evening after evening, Bilodo picked at his food, barely touching whatever was offered him – and Tania had to confess that the menu was enough to discourage all gastronomical ambitions. She suggested he share her salad, but he repeated that he wasn't hungry. Tania wanted him to regain his strength, so she kept up a flow of encouraging words, insisting that he should at least eat his dessert. Bilodo removed the plastic lid concealing the sweet of the day, a slice of lemon tart only distantly related to the magnificent concoction, served under the same name, that Mr Martinez produced at the Madelinot. Bilodo's tart, as it happened, was shop-bought and canary yellow in colour.

'Lemon tart! Your favourite dessert,' observed Tania with feigned enthusiasm.

'Really?' said Bilodo. 'I don't remember that.'

Lifting the slice of tart, he sniffed at it with one sceptical nostril. As she watched him, Tania suddenly remembered what Justine Tao had told her about sensory memory – a mere smell could suffice to cause the click! Wasn't there a risk that the lemony scent of the tart would remind Bilodo of the gentle citrus fragrance that perfumed Ségolène's haiku?

'Give me that tart!' she cried out.

Tania snatched the dangerous pastry from his hands. Unable to think of a more effective way to make it disappear, she devoured it in three mouthfuls. Swallowing with some difficulty, she noticed that Bilodo was gaping at her in amazement.

'I adore lemon tart,' she explained, trying to justify her fit of gluttony. 'It's my favourite dessert.'

'You said it was mine,' said Bilodo, surprised.

'I said that? I meant to say it was mine, of course. I can't resist a lemon tart,' Tania confessed. 'But you, you hate it. In fact, you're allergic to citrus fruit.'

'Whew, thanks for warning me.'

'What you love are cream puffs. They're your guilty pleasure,' Tania declared categorically. 'I'll bring you some tomorrow. But first you have to eat, at least your soup.'

'All right, but only because you want me to,' Bilodo conceded.

He thrust a spoon into his soup and began to swirl it around the bowl. Tania relaxed a little. She felt a vague urge to vomit. 'I'll have to be more careful,' she thought, counting herself lucky that Bilodo had swallowed, without flinching, the whopper about his citrus allergy – she felt she'd come close to disaster. On the other hand, there was every reason to hope: Bilodo didn't remember that he was mad about lemon tart, a sign that his amnesia remained as deep as ever.

It was the thirtieth of October, and Tania's footsteps echoed in the now empty apartment on rue des Hêtres. The movers had quickly cleared everything out. All that remained were two boxes that Tania would take with her when she left. One of them held certain personal effects of Bilodo's, which she planned to disperse around her apartment so that he would feel a little more 'at home'. The other box contained the totality of his poetic correspondence with Ségolène, as well as his other papers and those of Grandpré. Tania had considered burning all that, but, restrained by a sort of superstitious doubt, she hadn't been able to steel herself to do it. In the end, she'd decided to entrust the box and its explosive contents to Noémie, who would keep it in her own apartment, out of harm's way.

Tania was just giving the floors a final sweep when she heard the clack of the letterbox. Anxiety froze her for a few seconds. Then, peeking cautiously into the foyer, she was relieved to discover that the post wasn't a letter from Guadeloupe but a large envelope from the publishing house to which Bilodo had submitted the collection of Grandpré's poems. Inside the envelope was a contract for the publication of the manuscript *Enso*, together with a note from the editor. The latter expressed his keen desire to publish *Enso*; pointing out that nearly two months had passed without a reply to his telephone message of the twenty-ninth of August, he was, he wrote, taking the liberty of sending the enclosed contract, and he asked Grandpré to let him know quickly what his intentions were. Tania was tempted to imitate Grandpré's handwriting and sign the contract, but she discarded the idea, fearing that at some future time the published work might fall into Bilodo's hands and evoke some undesirable memories. Refusing to mortgage the future like that, Tania put the contract in the box containing the haiku. Then, leaving behind Bilodo's past as well as his ghosts, she left the apartment on rue des Hêtres with the firm resolve of never returning there again.

It was Halloween evening in the hospital. To enliven the atmosphere, pumpkins had been placed more or less everywhere, and the staff had organized a trick-or-treat itinerary for the child cancer sufferers in the oncology department. When she entered Bilodo's room, Tania found him distributing treats to a pack of young, leukemic vampires and other pint-sized monsters. For the occasion, he'd found a way to make himself a mummy costume out of toilet paper. Tania was touched to see him laugh, plainly having fun with the little patients. 'He'd make a good father,' she told herself, ovulating at the thought.

With a red carnation stuck in his buttonhole, Gaston Grandpré was lying on the flooded asphalt. It was just after the accident, in the steady downpour. The dying Grandpré fixed his eyes on Tania's and spoke in an evanescent voice: 'Swirling like water...against rugged rocks...time goes around and around...'

Grandpré hiccupped strangely, and the flabbergasted Tania realized that he was laughing. It was a hoarse, ghostly laugh. Grandpré was laughing as though at a painful joke. Then he stopped, strangled by a coughing fit. The light went out of his eyes. He expired. The clenched fingers of his right hand loosened, releasing their grip on a blood-stained envelope. Tania had just enough time to see that this was a letter addressed to Ségolène before it slid into the gutter, where a stream of reddish water flowed. Borne along to a storm drain, the letter swirled around for an instant and then was swallowed up into the bowels of the earth...and Tania awoke, dismayed by her morbid dream.

Shortly afterwards, in the shower, Tania absentmindedly dropped her bar of soap. Bending down to pick it up, she yielded to the fascination of the water that swirled around her feet before vanishing down the drain and thought again about her dream – about the bloody letter the sewer had sucked down, and about the dying man's enigmatic words:

> Swirling like water
> against rugged rocks,
> time goes around and around

Those words were not unknown to her. They constituted the opening haiku in *Enso*, Grandpré's

102

collection of poems. Apparently, the incident with the publication contract had given rise to her troubling dream. It was meaningless, Tania decided, but she couldn't manage to remain entirely convinced; on the contrary, in spite of herself, she had a feeling that the meaning of that cryptic poem was a matter of vital importance.

13

New brainstorming sessions with Justine Tao failed to allow Bilodo to reconnect with his past – much to Tania's satisfaction. Only the ceaselessly embellished tale she told him about the halcyon days of their love was capable of quenching his existential thirst. Physically, however, Bilodo was making a rapid recovery. He was already endeavouring to move his broken leg. In November, he was deemed ready for physiotherapy. He gave it all he had. Three weeks later, he was roaming through the corridors on his crutches, escaping from his room at a snail's pace. Weary of mouldering in the hospital, Bilodo clamoured for permission to leave. His doctor, finally yielding, released him, but not before making him promise not to set foot in a post office again, for any reason, before March. Bilodo had to continue his therapy and undergo other examinations, but in all other respects he was free.

Tania had seldom felt more nervous than on the fourteenth of December, the day of Bilodo's liberation, while sitting in the back seat of the taxi that was taking them 'home'. She helped him climb the exterior staircase and then led him into the apartment they'd supposedly begun to share eight months before. For greater plausibility, Tania had placed some of Bilodo's things here and there. Propped on his crutches, Bilodo surveyed the living room. With the exception of Bill, who was propelling himself through the water in his fishbowl, Bilodo obviously recognized nothing. Tania led him into the kitchen and continued to the bathroom, where she'd carefully laid out his toilet articles. Next she showed him the minuscule guest room, which was furnished with a sofa-bed, and then escorted him to the final room.

'Our bedroom,' she said.

The space was filled with sunlight. Tania had repainted it and added a second chest of drawers, into which she'd put Bilodo's underwear and other folded items of clothing. She opened the wardrobe and showed him his hanging garments as well as his postman's uniforms.

'Very nice,' said Bilodo, a little dejectedly.

'Is this all right?' asked Tania, afraid of having neglected some crucial detail.

'It's all fine. I'm happy to be back home. It's just that...I was hoping it would jog my memory a bit, but I don't remember anything about it. Nothing at all.'

'That's normal,' said Tania, indicating that Bilodo shouldn't worry.

Tania prepared their supper. Bilodo ate in relative silence. Apologizing for being so uncommunicative, he confessed that he was concerned about what would happen next. Money wasn't a problem; the compensation he was receiving from his salary insurance freed him from all pecuniary worries.

What Bilodo found particularly bothersome was the question of how he was going to occupy himself during his convalescence. He explained that work was among the things he valued most in life, and that the prospect of such a long period of idleness made him uncomfortable. What would he do with himself?

'Get better and get well,' Tania asserted. 'That's the only thing that matters.'

After supper, they put some logs in the fireplace and watched television. Sensing that Bilodo was as nervous as she was, Tania tried to relax them both by copiously filling their wine glasses, but the tension only increased as bedtime approached. Tania was simultaneously excited and fearful, like a teenager preparing to 'do it' for the first time. Bilodo, meanwhile, kept flicking between the channels, manifesting no desire whatsoever to move on to serious matters, and seeing that time was passing, Tania decided to take the initiative before she was too drunk: 'It's late. Let's go to bed,' she whispered.

'Yes,' Bilodo replied, turning off the telly. 'But I have a favour to ask. Would it bother you if I slept in the guest room?'

'...'

'This is all so new to me. I'm a little confused,' he pleaded.

Stoically facing this disappointment, Tania assured him that she understood. They performed their ablutions and then bade each other good night while standing at their respective doors. Tania fell onto her bed, satisfied, despite everything, that this crucial day, the day of Bilodo's 'return', had passed without a hitch. It had ended on a somewhat discouraging note, but after all, it seemed normal that Bilodo would need time to adapt. Tania consoled herself with the thought that the nights to come would be all the hotter.

The following evening, Tania ran a fragrant bath for Bilodo, lit a few candles and put on some atmospheric music. Nevertheless, he cited his aching leg as an excuse for preferring to go to bed alone. The shadow of a doubt passed over Tania, but she respected Bilodo's modesty.

The evening after that, Bilodo went to the guest room and closed the door without offering so much as a token excuse, as if the matter were resolved from then on. Disenchanted, Tania had to admit that something was wrong.

'Bilodo?' she called, tapping gently on the door of the guest room.

'Yes?' he answered from the other side.

'I'd just like...to say good night.'

'Thanks, you too.'

And then silence. Tania leaned her back against the door. She had naively imagined that planting Bilodo in her home would be enough to bring a passion that had been sprouting for so long into full flower, but the reality was different; two weeks after his arrival, they were still sleeping in separate rooms. Nevertheless, Tania kept trying to excite his senses. She went to the beauty salon and got herself a vampish hairdo, she went to the nail salon and got herself some pretty fingernails, she scented herself with a new perfume supposed to fire masculine desire. She bought a scandalous bestseller and deliberately left it lying about more or less everywhere, and she did her yoga routines in the middle of the living room, attempting to impress Bilodo with her flexibility. But these erotic signals had no apparent effect. Raising the audacity bar a notch, Tania formed the habit of leaving the door ajar while she had a bath, hoping that Bilodo would see that as an invitation to enter the bathroom, or at least to peek at her through the opening in the door, but not so much as an eyeball appeared in the crack – it was enough to make her chew up her soap! She updated her supply of lingerie to include some alluring nighties, in which she paraded around right under Bilodo's nose, but such manoeuvres seemed to arouse in him nothing but embarrassment: he'd avert his eyes and take refuge in the guest room, to Tania's great chagrin. She was reduced to listening to him snoring on the other side of the door while she stared at her beautiful, useless fingernails.

Bilodo's state of mind was hard to define. He didn't seem unhappy. He smiled frequently. If asked how he was doing, he said everything was fine. But for all that he remained distant and laconic. When Tania came home from work, she'd find him playing a video game, from which he would disconnect only reluctantly. She assumed that his inactivity was weighing on him, that he felt bored. From time to time, like someone emerging from a trance, he'd eye her up and down, bizarrely, as if he could read her. Those strange looks gave Tania the jitters and nourished her dread of being unmasked; they haunted her even in her dreams.

'What are you complaining about, Tania Schumpf? Don't you have what you wanted?' she would think, reasoning with herself when she started to get the blues. Besides, Tania agreed with her inner voice: all was not so dark, things could be worse, and in fact, the glum atmosphere was sometimes punctuated with happy moments. For Christmas, Bilodo presented her with a bracelet of finely worked silver, and she gave him a chain with a little locket containing her photograph: 'So you'll never forget me,' she whispered as she put the chain around his neck. After that, he was more than willing to watch *The Remains of the Day*, one of Tania's favourite films; she'd chosen it deliberately, because it best symbolized their relationship. Tania knew the film by heart, but she savoured every frame as though for the first time, overjoyed to let herself be carried along by the plot in the company of Bilodo, and to feel him quiver at the same moments she did. In the end, when Stevens, the butler, stood in the rain and waved his final farewell to Miss Kenton as the bus carried her away, both of them – Tania and Bilodo – burst into tears, which gave Tania an exhilarating feeling of complicity.

A delicious moment, but brief, and the following day Bilodo fell back into apathy. Video game, supper, solo beddy-byes: it had taken only a few days for that monotonous routine, that nocturnal apartheid, to become established. Tania's confidence was shaken; what would it take to stimulate this impassive postman's ardour? Was it going to be necessary for her to get the Canada Post logo tattooed on some part of her body?

Now ready to consider last-resort solutions, Tania purchased some of the Haitian love philtre whose aphrodisiac virtues her friend Noémie had extolled. That very evening, finding Bilodo no more amorous than usual, she poured a triple dose into his beef stroganoff. After supper, Tania put on some bossa nova and asked Bilodo for a dance. She didn't let herself be discouraged by his embarrassed refusal and pulled him against her. Swaying languorously to the rhythm of the music, she put her arms around his neck and kissed him – tried to kiss him, that is, for the speechless Bilodo allowed it to happen without any reaction. Tania was forced to recognize the sad, obvious fact; every part of him remained stony, except for his member, which she realized was desperately flaccid.

Detaching himself from Tania's arms, Bilodo notified her that he was going to bed.

'Wait,' she said, grabbing one of his hands and holding him back. 'Why are you so distant?'

'I'm tired,' he offered as a pretext.

'Bilodo, I love you,' she declared fervently.

'So do I, but I feel empty,' he replied, his eyes dead. 'I believed my thoughts would clear up when I came back home, but I've still got this big blank spot inside my head...I'm a stranger in my own skin.'

Bilodo withdrew. Hearing him close that bloody guest-room door one more time, Tania sighed bitterly and set about finishing the bottle of wine by herself. Shortly afterwards, taking advantage of one of those brief moments of amazing lucidity that drunkenness sometimes provides, she admitted that she'd made a stupid mistake by trying to entice Bilodo into her bed when he clearly wasn't ready for it. Apparently she'd been going about things the wrong way from the beginning; it was Bilodo's heart she must address first, not his senses. Only later, once Bilodo was re-endowed with his emotions and his ability to love, would the moment come to let the flesh exult.

Before anything else, it was Bilodo's soul that Tania had to touch.

Returning home from her job that snowy New Year's Eve, Tania was pleasantly surprised to find the video game turned off. Bilodo was sitting at the kitchen table. He was doing calligraphy.

Tania felt a knot in her stomach. Was this the result of one of the flashbacks Justine Tao had talked about? Was this a sign that he was regaining his memory?

Bilodo had taken out the pens and the exercise book Tania had used while learning the basics of calligraphy two years earlier. In all probability, he'd discovered the things in the back of the drawer where she'd put them and then forgotten them.

'I didn't know you liked calligraphy,' said Bilodo.

'I do, a lot,' Tania felt obliged to affirm.

'It's interesting. I love it.'

Flashback or not, the damage was already done. Lines of Gothic letters, one after the other, marched down the page, the fruits of Bilodo's meticulous work. Unable to come up with a pretext she could use to dissuade him from continuing, Tania took a seat at the table, chose a pen, and started to form beautiful letters too.

That was the way they ended the year, enjoying a delightful evening, embellishing sheets of paper with elegant handwriting.

14

A new year began. The platonic cohabitation dragged on. According to Justine Tao, the sensation of emptiness that Bilodo felt was normal in the circumstances. She predicted that he would recover his affective balance at the same time as his memory. Now this memory recall was precisely what Tania was trying hard to avoid, and so if the shrink was right, Tania was helping to reinforce Bilodo's emotional block, and as long as his amnesia continued, he would remain incapable of falling in love – a paradoxical situation, if not a circle of the most vicious kind. It was one thing to reinvent the past; it was quite another to create love out of nothing. Where to start? How could she touch Bilodo's temporarily disabled heart?

As soon as he was able to move around without crutches, Bilodo asked to see the scene of his accident. Dr Tao had advised him to visit systematically the places that had been familiar or significant to him in the past, and Bilodo wished to follow her recommendations. As Tania certainly had no intention of standing with him outside his former apartment, she instead led Bilodo instead to a previously selected street corner, where she pointed at some random patch of asphalt that naturally reminded him of nothing at all. Two days

later, Bilodo conceived a desire to go to the restaurant where they had met, the place where their
love began. Tania congratulated herself for never
having mentioned the name of the Madelinot,
because letting Bilodo set foot in there again was
totally out of the question. She contacted Noémie,
who without too much balking agreed to perform
a rather unusual service for her.

'Hello, young lovers!' Noémie cried out joyously
the next day, welcoming them like regular customers
to Café Scaramouche, on rue Saint-Denis, where she
worked as a waitress.

Skilfully playing her role, Noémie pretended to
know Bilodo well; she evoked, with perfectly feigned
nostalgia, the happy period when he frequented the
café and courted her dear friend Tania. Bilodo was
completely taken in, and Noémie, who having sight-
ed this rare bird for the first time, called Tania that
evening to share her impressions.

'A good-looking man, a bit withdrawn, but sexy
in his way. I'm reserving my final verdict, but I'm
tempted to give him an A.'

Which, in Noémie Code, stood for 'Acceptable',
a grade less disappointing than it might seem to
anyone unfamiliar with Noémie's stratospheric
standards for rating persons of the male gender, and
in fact the highest mark on a scale with only three
levels: A for Acceptable, B for Bastard and C for
Creep. There was no doubt that Bilodo's extraterres-
trial charm had worked on her.

'Thanks for your help,' Tania told her gratefully.

'Don't thank me,' replied Noémie. 'I know you're crazy about that guy, but don't ask me to approve of what you're doing. You won't be able to say I didn't warn you.'

Tania, slightly ashamed, hung up. Questioning the morality of her acts one more time, she asked herself if she had the right to manipulate Bilodo the way she'd been doing for the past few months. Did love really excuse everything? Her scruples disappeared instantaneously the following day, when Bilodo revealed his intention to go to the Depot. He wanted to renew his acquaintance with his forgotten colleagues, a project that forced Tania to tap into her emergency supply of self-control and expend a goodly portion. She could have no doubt that Robert would happily annihilate the brandnew, beautiful past she had striven so hard to create for Bilodo. Hard-pressed, Tania reminded Bilodo that his doctor had forbidden him to enter a post office before his convalescence was complete. She managed to dissuade him with that argument, but she had no doubt the matter would come up again; and other, equally pernicious initiatives must be anticipated as well. A varied menu of catastrophic scenarios flashed through Tania's fertile imagination; the most calamitous of them were related to the arrival of the first day of March, a date which had once appeared remote but suddenly seemed close at hand. What would happen when Bilodo's sick leave was over? Wouldn't everything go right down the drain the moment he stepped into a post-sorting facility again?

Enjoying his recovered autonomy, Bilodo had been doing a lot of walking, lately even exploring the adjacent neighbourhoods. Tania feared that his peregrinations might soon take him all the way to Saint-Janvier, where there was a good chance he would instinctively retrace his former postal route and eventually end up in front of Grandpré's old apartment or the Madelinot. In order to point Bilodo's walks towards less perilous destinations, Tania planned to give him errand lists designed to take him in diametrically opposite directions, but he wouldn't be able to help himself: in the end, his internal compass would guide him back to Saint-Janvier.

One morning Tania saw Bilodo engaged in an odd activity; he was repeatedly going up and down the outside staircase in the bitter cold, nearly fifteen degrees below zero. Fahrenheit. He explained that he was training so that he'd be in good shape when he returned to work. Two days later, hearing the kettle whistling in the kitchen, Tania found a glassy-eyed Bilodo steaming open his own post, an indubitable echo of his former vice as an inquisitive postman. This misty episode was but the first in a series of increasingly alarming incidents. The following Saturday, while they were out shopping on rue Sainte-Catherine, a beautiful black woman passed them, and Tania saw Bilodo turn around, his eyes following the woman, and on his face the somnambulistic expression Tania dreaded: this time, she thought, he was surely having one of those flashbacks that Justine Tao had predicted. Less than an hour later, Bilodo froze in front of a shop window displaying Far Eastern merchandise, including a red kimono that fascinated him. 'I think I used to wear something like that,' he said in a toneless voice. Keeping a cool head, Tania confirmed that he had in fact owned a red dressing gown, a rather uncomfortable garment he'd ended up giving to a charitable organization. Bilodo accepted this explanation and spoke of the kimono no more, but from that point on, Tania noticed, his attention was magnetized by any red article of clothing. Fortunately, Christmas had already been and gone; otherwise, Bilodo would probably have slipped into a trance every time he saw a Santa Claus, an apparition doubly dangerous because its beard could have reminded him of Gaston Grandpré's.

One Sunday morning in mid January, Tania found Bilodo watching a television travelogue about Guadeloupe. 'What a beautiful place. We should go on holiday there,' he said, filled with wonder.

Quickly changing the channel, Tania settled on a documentary whose subject was Iceland and resorted to praising the tectonic splendours of that resolutely northern country. Similar pirouettes and mental contortions were often necessary, and her acrobatic management of the imponderable became more taxing with each passing day. And so, complicated by the constant vigilance to which Bilodo's unpredictable reminiscences compelled her, the subtle task of re-programming his heart posed a greater and greater challenge for Tania. Flashbacks popped up everywhere, like demons on springs – apparently the forerunners of a major reflux of memory – and Tania was forced to acknowledge that the situation was spiralling out of her control. Assessing the scale of the levy that the events of the past several months had placed on her nerves, she felt drained of all strength and frightfully alone. 'What a fine mess you've got yourself into, Tania Schumpf,' her inner voice rebuked her. 'You're as tense as a piano string. You live in fear. If this continues, you're going to snap.' And in fact, collapse seemed imminent. Tania felt an urgent need for a pause, for a moment of respite, no matter how brief, so that she could recharge her batteries and renew her courage. But how could she allow herself to lower her guard for an instant in that city, rife with dangers, where the perfidious past was lurking everywhere?

She knew she couldn't defy fate indefinitely, and her stress was skyrocketing, hoisting her to such levels of anxiety that she always came back down weeping. She was careful to hide those tears, not wanting Bilodo to witness them, but one evening when she thought he was already in bed, he came into the kitchen and found her silently sobbing. Distressed at seeing her like that, Bilodo assumed it was his fault and asked her to forgive him for still being an amnesiac. He swore he would make greater efforts to recover his memory, an oath that only added to Tania's torment.

'I can do better,' he declared, looking resolute. 'I'll come to love you as much as before. If I keep on trying, it's sure to work in the end.'

And that – that was the worst of all – what could be more depressing than Bilodo's absolute sincerity, his unconditional commitment? Seeing him struggling so hard to love her without success, how could she not find herself pathetic, how could she not believe herself the most wretched of women? 'It's hopeless, Tania Schumpf,' she thought, despairing of ever being able to arouse the least glimmer of authentic love in Bilodo.

The following night, as she passed Bilodo's door on the way to the toilet, Tania heard him talking in his room. She pricked up her ears, thinking that he was talking on the telephone, but his tone wasn't conversational. Plucking up her courage, she half-opened the door. Bilodo was talking in his sleep: 'Cinnamon, saffron...*malangas* and *carambolas*,' he muttered.

He was apparently dreaming about exotic spices and fruits, but the particular order in which he spoke the words sounded familiar to Tania's ear. She recognized where they came from: one of Ségolène's haiku. 'He's reciting her poems,' she realized, horrified.

'I dream about waking up...by your side...into a bright dawn...surely the most beautiful...of all mornings in the world,' Bilodo sighed.

Tania felt her heart break into pieces.

'I was talking in my sleep? What did I say?' Bilodo asked in surprise. They were having lunch.

'I couldn't quite make it out,' Tania lied.

'I don't remember a thing,' Bilodo declared.

'Thank goodness,' Tania thought, all too aware that this was, at best, a reprieve. That sudden effusion of poetry surely marked the beginning of the end. Ségolène's haiku were floating back up to the surface, already brushing against Bilodo's consciousness; it wouldn't be long before he actively remembered them, and then he'd have a thousand questions. 'How can I answer him?' she thought desolately, yielding to an attack of fatalism. Wasn't it time to admit defeat and acknowledge Ségolène's supremacy? What was the point of this obstinate struggle against the spellbinding charm of the Guadeloupian woman and the sovereign power of her haiku, which alone seemed capable, through their seventeen syllables' unfathomable magic, of moving Bilodo's heart?

Suddenly, Tania was caused to reflect; something that moved Bilodo's heart – wasn't that exactly what she was looking for?

The solution could only be poetic.

Tania would use haiku to give Bilodo a kind of emotional electroshock. The poems would act as romantic defibrillators, which with a little luck would restart his stalled heart. It was risky, but it might work. In any case, it was worth trying.

15

Drawn with a finger
on a frosty windowpane
a sun is smiling

It certainly wasn't as dazzling as one of Ségolène's poems, but at least it was something. Before leaving for work, Tania slipped the haiku under Bilodo's door and then fled on tiptoe, aware that she had just gone for broke. At first, she'd thought about copying out a few of the Guadeloupian's poems, but the idea of adding plagiarism to the list of her crimes repelled her. Were she ever to succeed in touching Bilodo's heart, she wanted it to be by her own merits, and thanks to her own words, however humble they might be. Therefore, Tania proposed to offer Bilodo only poems of her own composition – which would, among other things, lessen the risk of evoking the spectre of Ségolène, for should Bilodo eventually recall the island woman's haiku, he would naturally attribute them to Tania.

The day seemed interminable. Not knowing what to expect, Tania sometimes assumed the worst and sometimes the best. That evening, when she finally arrived home, Bilodo gave her an enthusiastic welcome. The pretty little poem he'd found under his door captivated him, intrigued him. There was no indication that he had remembered Ségolène. Tania pretended that before Bilodo's accident it had been their charming habit, hers and his, to exchange poems in Japanese style, and she instructed Bilodo in the workings of a *renku*. He was prodigiously interested and proclaimed the whole idea 'brilliant'.

The following morning, Tania found a carefully calligraphed haiku under her door:

> Bill's in his bubble
> waiting for manna
> dreaming of infinite ponds

> Thus we go along
> not knowing that our pathways
> are already traced

> It's snakes and ladders
> everything's hanging
> on the next roll of the dice

> Sitting on my hat
> a little bird, bright and fat
> sings his songs for you

> Weary of desert confines
> I lie down at last
> in your oasis

Endlessly echoed
between two mirrors
our faces: the absolute

The situation was strangely inspiring. Every evening, Tania slipped a new poem under Bilodo's door, and the next morning she'd find a response lying across her threshold. It was a daily challenge, thrown down again and again, that filled the hours and usurped all thought, but it was also a source of happiness, of the slightly paradoxical joy of creation, with its retinue of apprehensions and doubts, followed by euphoria when at last, under deadline pressure, the daily tercet came to fruition. Bilodo hadn't had a flashback since poetry had once again become his soul's natural way of getting some fresh air. His delight in expressing himself broke through his habitual reserve. Bilodo would smile, and for Tania it was – every time – like a waft of oxygen, a grace that allowed her to forget for a few moments the approaching, fateful date of the first of March, the sword of Damocles hanging over her. Hoping to gain time, she suggested to Bilodo that he apply for an extension of his sick leave, but he swept this idea aside: 'I can barely wait to start working. I miss walking my route,' he replied.

Unshakable, he explained that it was a question not only of pride, but also of pleasure. By all appearances, not even a nuclear attack would make him postpone his return to the postal service any longer, and Tania had to resign herself; her postman's postal zeal was too great, she couldn't immobilize him any longer...unless she broke his other leg?

'Suppose we move to Germany?' she blurted out impulsively, one evening when they were doing calligraphy.

Wasn't that, in fact, the ideal solution? To put some distance between Bilodo and Montreal...to flee that overly familiar city, teeming with baleful memories...to take him somewhere far away...to scrape off the scales of the past and start a new life there...

Carried away by that exciting prospect, Tania announced her desire to see her native Bavaria again. She made the case that Munich was lovely at that time of year, with its snow-covered cathedrals. They would explore the cultural riches of the ancient city and follow Kandinsky's traces in the borough of Schwabing; they would eat in some of the many beer halls, typical establishments where the customers contended in epic tarot games and quaffed hearty brews served out by waitresses in traditional costume. Then, as a digestive aid, they'd go skiing in the Alps!

Anticipating Bilodo's objections, Tania committed herself to teaching him German and assured him he wouldn't have any trouble finding gainful employment over there: her father, a vice-president at Siemens, would use his connections to get Bilodo a job as a postman.

'All you have to do is apply for a sabbatical leave,' she pointed out. 'If you don't like Bavaria, we'll come back to Montreal.'

Bilodo admitted that this spontaneous proposal was not without appeal. Encouraged, Tania told him they could live in her Uncle Reinhardt's country house on the shore of Lake Starnberg, a romantic spot she'd often visited as a child during the sacred summer-holiday season. She added that Lufthansa offered a daily flight to Munich, so they could fly there anytime, and soon. But this was to assume a spontaneity foreign to Bilodo's nature, and he suddenly became reluctant. He acknowledged that it was a fine project, but he suggested they take the time to consider it more fully – wouldn't it be more reasonable to make plans for an exploratory trip to Bavaria during the holiday period next July? Unwilling to upset Bilodo, Tania chose not to insist; she would polish her arguments and return to the charge at the appropriate moment. Because she nevertheless wanted to keep the idea alive in him, she put a tourist guide to Bavaria on the coffee table and selected a new wallpaper for the computer screen: a view of Lake Starnberg and the Alps. After doing that, she took down the calendar and hid it at the back of a drawer, forbidding herself to think about the first of March.

That night, Tania dreamt she was strolling about in Munich with Bilodo. They visited the old city, they promenaded in the Odeonsplatz, and then, while the

For something new was, in fact, shining in Bilodo's eyes – a sparkle heretofore unseen. Tania thought she detected in it a new feeling that transcended friendship, a feeling she dared not name. Had a few heartfelt haiku sufficed to accomplish what had adamantly resisted two years of painstaking effort?

Was it, at long last, love?

She mustn't say it too loud, lest the word's mere vibration shatter that crystalline magic, she mustn't make any move liable to weaken the miracle, and above all, she mustn't rush anything...

Deep inside my eyes
you see yours looking at you:
my eyes, filled with you

For that's where I live
deep inside your eyes
no existence outside them

Compared to your eyes
the purest emeralds lose
luminosity

Deep inside your eyes
I dissolve, I flow through you
you're inundated

You stream in my veins
overflow my heart
I will love you for ever

And as she read those last words, Tania was overcome by a peculiar combination of bliss and anguish. It seemed to her that she could never be happier, and never more uneasy. So was that what it was like, true love?

16

You are the end of my night
you my rising sun
you my sacred dawn

All I can offer
are a few dewdrops
will you be content with them?

To fly your colours
to fight in your name
I have no other desire

Can I ever be worthy
of so high a love?
Let's exchange our hearts
our souls are already twins
conjoined everlastingly

Nothing will separate us
time will bleach my bones
commingled with yours

And must we then wait
for Death to take us?
As long as you held me close...

Tania had never dared to enter the room across the hall, fearing a new erotic defeat, but she soon had good reason to hope for the end of the apartheid: Bilodo's attitude was rapidly evolving, as demonstrated by the increasingly intimate tone of his haiku:

I'll adorn your neck
with pearls of the rain
and dress you all in flowers

It's with your kisses
and not your roses
I desire to be covered

My bold hand shall venture forth
on the virgin snow
of your naked hip

At night in my thoughts
I step across your threshold
slip into your bed

So that's the reason
why I wake up so often
astonished by you

Do you dream sometimes
of departing your body

and visiting mine?

I plan to invent
a new religion
and its goddess shall be you

I know a temple
where the Holy of Holies
is silky and warm

From intimacy to desire there was but a step, which Bilodo finally seemed to have taken. It was causing him insomnia. At night, through their shared wall, Tania would hear him tossing and turning in his bed. Then he'd get up and tour the apartment. He'd wander from room to room, making the floor creak in front of Tania's door, where he'd stand still for long moments. She could imagine him, his hand raised, not daring to knock. Having recently found herself before a similar closed door, Tania enjoyed this reversal of their situations with a touch of guilty pleasure: being on the inside of the door was decidedly more comfortable. Her desire to open it to Bilodo was strong, but her inner voice commanded her to remain under her duvet. The new flame that had been lit by the poetry – Tania decided she should let it burn a little while longer, until Bilodo could no longer stand the heat and finally found the courage to come in. Then and only then would she give herself to him.

A beach could accommodate
our swells, our surging
billows, our high tides

I would be the sea
my waves caress you
submerging you in kisses

I enter your skin
swim around in your water
dive into your heat

Let yourself founder
slip into my deepest depths
abandon that ship

A sublime shipwreck
am I touching the bottom
or is it heaven?

Plunge into my soft abyss
explore my secret
Mariana Trench

Tania didn't have to wait long. On the morning of
the sixteenth of February, a few minutes before her
alarm clock went off, she had the sensation of being
observed, opened her eyes, and saw Bilodo standing

at the foot of her bed and staring at her vacuously. How long had he been looming there, watching her sleep?

'Here you are at last,' Tania murmured.

Looking shattered, like someone suddenly snatched out of a trance, Bilodo fled the room. Tania put on her dressing gown and joined him in the living room, where he was gaping at Bill with eyes no less watery than the fish's own. Bilodo turned to Tania – his face displaying the expression of a hunted animal – and apologized for having awakened her. Stepping softly, she moved closer to him. Bilodo was shaking. Tania raised herself on tiptoe and placed upon his lips a kiss charged with static electricity, which made them both flinch. Caught in the act, Tania dared not repeat it and instead laid her head on Bilodo's shoulder. She pressed her chest against his and felt his heart beating hard. Or was it her own heart, she wondered, pounding away for both of them? Wasn't the excitement she thought she read in Bilodo's eyes merely a reflection of her own? It was at this point that he took her in his arms and kissed her. A genuine kiss, a desperate kiss, which moved Tania to her innermost depths, and to which she responded passionately, emancipated from time, transported to some voluptuous elsewhere.

'I love you,' Bilodo breathed.

'I love you too.'

'You're sure?'

'Absolutely.'

'How do you do it?' he asked, suddenly worried. 'How can you be certain that you love me?'

'My heart tells me so. It's got a little voice, and it whispers that we were made to be together.'

'You could have met another man, one you would have loved as much as me.'

'It wouldn't have been the same. My heart would have told me he wasn't the right one.'

'Our paths might never have crossed. What would you have done?'

'I would have looked for you until I found you. But I don't have to, because here you are.'

'Yes, here I am. But what would you have done if you hadn't been able to bring me back to life after the accident?'

'Don't say that...'

Tania cut off Bilodo's existential apprehensions by sealing his lips with hers. For his part, the newly enterprising Bilodo began to caress her through her dressing gown, but she gently tempered his ardour.

'Tonight,' Tania whispered, wanting the pleasure to last.

Tania's customers in the Petit Malin complimented her on her animation, her energy, her radiant beauty. 'Thanks,' she answered, with Mona Lisa-like reserve. In her distraction, she licked her lips, still tasting Bilodo's kisses. She had detached herself from his arms with difficulty, assuring him that they would continue their tender encounter that evening. He'd regretfully let her go and promised to prepare something special for their supper. Tania couldn't keep herself from anticipating the marvellous moments that were waiting for her. After a bubble bath and an excellent meal, she would deploy her charms and draw Bilodo into her bed, and there they would catapult themselves to those ecstatic heights where, it was said, two lovers become one. She would make Bilodo succumb with pleasure, and she'd share with him every spasm of ravishing carnal agony. Her long months of patience would be compensated, and thus would begin a new era, a full-blown romantic relationship, a period of exquisite promise.

At midday, while serving customers who were on their way north to do some skiing, Tania had an idea: Noémie had the use of a chalet in the Laurentides owned by her mother – Tania and her friend had spent some wonderful ski weekends there. The house stood in the middle of the forest. It was an ideal refuge, isolated and outside of time...once reached by telephone, Noémie voiced no objection to lending Tania her chalet; Tania had only to pick up the keys. She promised to do so the following day, certain as she was that Bilodo wouldn't say no. That place in the woods was a providential *sanctum* where they could love each other in total freedom by the fireside, a haven of peace where Tania could calmly ponder the possibilities of allaying the curse of the first of March which still hung over them. Energized by pure air and wild nature, she'd be able to persuade Bilodo to move to Bavaria, or to somewhere else – in any case, she'd find a way to avoid romantic apocalypse.

'It's me,' Tania sang out, crossing the threshold of the apartment early that evening.

She was surprised when she got no response from Bilodo. Noticing that his overcoat wasn't in the entrance hall, she assumed he was out running errands. In the dining room, Tania found the table set for a candlelight supper, a state of affairs that augured very well. Then she ventured into the kitchen and understood that something was wrong. The refrigerator door was open, and fragments of broken crockery lay on the floor. The ingredients of a half-prepared meal were scattered over the counter. An intense scent of citrus permeated the kitchen, coming from a bowl that contained the grated zest of several lemons. An open recipe book lay next to the bowl. When she glanced at it, Tania realized that Bilodo had set about making a lemon tart.

'My God!' she exclaimed, remembering what Justine Tao had told her about the catalytic effect certain evocative smells could produce.

Struggling against panic, she telephoned Bilodo. He didn't answer. She sent him a text message, asking him where he was. Not long afterwards, his reply came: 'What have you done with Ségolène's haiku?' read the words on Tania's little screen. She sank down into a chair, crushed, because there could no longer be any doubt: Bilodo had remembered.

Distraught, Tania mashed the digital keys on her mobile phone, sending Bilodo text after text:

'Where are you, my love?'

'Come back, I'll explain everything!'

'Come back, I'm begging you...'

'Come back...'

Bilodo ignored her.

Outside the wind was howling. Tania shivered. She sat on the sofa, wrapped herself in a blanket, and waited.

She waited for Bilodo's return, preparing herself for a stormy showdown, straining to devise a minimally satisfactory explanation.

She waited, praying that he'd understand her distress and come back.

Dawn came, and still Bilodo had not returned.

17

Bilodo accepted the cup of coffee the flight attendant offered him and then fell to contemplating the Atlantic Ocean through his window. The plane had taken off at dawn, after an interminable night of waiting in the airport, where he'd been able to read the text messages sent to him by his so-called fiancée. Bilodo couldn't get over Tania's unbelievable treachery; he hadn't stopped fuming about it. To think, he'd believed he was in love with her! But that was before his memory had come back to him, before he'd realized the extent to which he'd been duped – it was before he'd remembered Ségolène, before his headlong dash had begun...

> As though suspended
> in an eternal morning
> I'm flying to her

Soon Bilodo would tread the sacred soil that had witnessed Ségolène's birth. 'I'm coming,' he kept repeating like a mantra, all the while knowing full well he could take absolutely nothing for granted. There was no self-deception involved: he knew he'd never be able to pass himself off as Grandpré. Besides, he had no intention of even trying to do so. On the contrary, he wanted to put an end to the entire charade. He would quite simply lay his love at Ségolène's feet, leave the rest up to her, and comply with her wishes.

> All my memories
> were buried inside
> the scent of a lemon tart

For this was how, while he was making that dessert for Tania – supposedly her favourite – everything had suddenly come back to him. The fragrance of the zested lemons had transfixed him, causing in his head a popcorn-like explosion of images that told the story of the past several years of his life.

It was the tale of a solitary boy, passionate about calligraphy, of a conscientious postman perhaps too curious for his own good. Amid the great mass of wasted paper he delivered in the course of his daily round, the thousands of soulless pages, now and again he found in his hand a personal letter, a very rare object these days, and so all the more fascinating. That letter in Bilodo's hand didn't immediately reach its addressee; he took it home with him and read it as if it were the latest episode in a serial that was significantly more fascinating than his own existence. A few of the many letters he purloined touched him in a particular way. Those were the poetic missives written by a Guadeloupian woman named Ségolène to a professor of literature named Gaston Grandpré:

My neighbour's macaw
grumbles jealously
hearing my canary sing

Fragmented clouds at sunset
the ragged canvas
of a phantom ship

Orion sparkles
mocking Jupiter
wind ploughs furrows in my hair

Those letters, each consisting of a single haiku, had immediately bewitched Bilodo, bringing him magnificent visions that contrasted with the ordinary drabness of his daily life. Enthralled by those little snatches of eternity, he'd fallen in love with Ségolène. For a long time, he had contented himself with secretly dreaming of her and worshipping her from afar, but then Grandpré's death had occurred, and it seemed the correspondence that had become so precious to Bilodo must die too. It was then that Bilodo, seeking a way to prevent the dissolution of the sole link connecting him to Ségolène, hit upon the brilliant idea of borrowing the identity of the deceased.

In his determination to pass himself off as Grandpré, Bilodo had stopped at nothing; he'd burgled the dead man's apartment and stolen his papers. Since he needed to compose poems that

could pass as authentic in Ségolène's eyes, Bilodo
had trained himself to imitate the late Grandpré's
handwriting and set about mastering the subtle art
of haiku. In order to identify himself more closely
with the deceased, Bilodo had rented his apartment
and moved not only into his rooms but also into his
clothes. Listening to Japanese music and living on
sushi, Bilodo had learned the basics of Zen philoso-
phy and written hundreds of disastrous haiku – until
the day when, wearing a red kimono he'd found in
a closet, he had at last experienced the sensation of
slipping into Grandpré's skin and written, in a single
access of inspiration, a poem that seemed worthy of
Ségolène.

Eleven days after Bilodo posted that haiku, a letter
from the Guadeloupian woman had arrived. It was a
poem that responded to his. It had worked! Ségolène
had fallen for it! And thus a strange period of epistolary happiness had begun; secluded in the dead man's
former residence, Bilodo had sent Ségolène a series
of rhapsodic haiku, to which she had replied with
increasing fervour.

Now, looking back, he saw that this was clearly
the period during which Tania had begun a series
of manoeuvres designed to win his heart. First she'd
been interested in the haiku he was writing, and then
she had taken up haiku-writing too. When she'd
suggested that they start a *renku*, he should have
suspected something, but he hadn't actually become
aware of Tania's feelings until the episode of the

stolen tanka, that dirty trick Robert had played on them. Intended for Ségolène, the poem had fallen into Robert's hands, and that was the way he'd discovered Bilodo's great romantic secret. Bilodo, desperate to recover his tanka, had confronted Robert and found himself obliged to strike him. An act for which his colleague had got his revenge by giving Tania a copy of the poem and so placing Bilodo in an embarrassing situation, which had degenerated after the young waitress grasped that she'd been played for a fool. Whereupon Bilodo had taken refuge in the private universe of his virtual relationship with Ségolène. Cut off from the world, he'd lived for months on little but fantasies, exploring with the beautiful Guadeloupian the multiple dimensions of a lyrical passion that carried them both to peaks of ecstasy.

Then, at the end of August, the tanka in which Ségolène announced her impending arrival had come...

Bilodo squirmed in his seat, reliving the torments into which that announcement had plunged him. For he'd been sure that Ségolène would see through the hoax the moment she saw him. Contemplating the inevitable revelation of his deception filled Bilodo with such despair that he had decided to hang himself. He'd escaped suicide only because, at the moment when the noose was tightening around his neck, Tania had paid him a surprise visit. It had been a truly unique moment, that face-to-face meeting with the young waitress on the balcony. Ultimately,

Bilodo had had the impression that something special was on the point of passing between them, and as he watched Tania walk away he'd felt a pang in his heart, not yet suspecting whom and what he was dealing with...The sweet and innocent Tania, so clever at dissembling her selfish schemes.

It was shortly after Tania's departure that the miracle had taken place.

Inadvertently glimpsing his reflection in a mirror, Bilodo could have sworn it was Grandpré's face staring out at him! Then he'd recognized his own features in those of the dead man, and he had realized that what he was actually looking at was the result of several months of hygiene neglect. Absorbed in his epistolary idyll, he'd been totally remiss in the care of his person, so much so that he had come to this; with his six-month beard, his long, tangled mass of hair and that red kimono on his back, he bore a striking resemblance to the deceased – so much so, he'd suddenly realized, that Ségolène might not notice a thing.

All at once, Bilodo had felt that it was in his power to reverse his fortune. Euphoric at the thought, he'd composed, in haiku form, a warm invitation to the beautiful Guadeloupian to come to Montreal. In his eagerness to post the poem, he'd gone out in spite of the storm. He'd run across the street towards the postbox that his old enemy Robert, accompanied by another postman, was in the process of emptying of its contents, and...

Bilodo had died that day. The great darkness had enveloped him.

And yet, six months later, here he was, sitting in an aeroplane, alive and well. Thanks to Tania – generous, hypocritical Tania. Bilodo would have liked to believe in the goodness of her intentions, but he just couldn't; it was now clear that Tania had revived him only in order to take possession of him. She'd manipulated his memory and odiously hijacked his love, providing him with a second life as a carefully programmed slave, fettering him to her desires. She had deceived him. She had taken advantage of him – so to hell with her!

Only Ségolène counted for him now.

'I'm coming,' Bilodo whispered, but at the same time aware that he was flying into an immense uncertainty. How had Ségolène interpreted the silence that had followed her last tanka? How would she receive Gaston Grandpré's unexpected replacement? Wasn't it highly likely that she would take him for a madman?

The cabin crew chief asked the passengers to prepare for their landing at Pointe-à-Pitre International Airport. Bilodo fastened his seatbelt; soon he'd know where he stood.

Dawn was breaking, and Bilodo still hadn't come home. The dining-room window filtered the sun's first rays. Tania opened the computer, logged onto the Internet and checked Bilodo's credit-card account. Her intuition was confirmed: he had indeed purchased an airline ticket to Guadeloupe. Tania had a vision of Bilodo clasping Ségolène to his bosom, afloat on the long waves of a turquoise sea – a nightmare that would soon become reality unless she could manage to stop it.

After hastily packing a travel bag, Tania made a beeline for the airport. The next flight to Pointe-à-Pitre wouldn't take off until one o'clock in the afternoon. Obliged to wait, Tania called Noémie, who agreed to take care of Bill, and then called the Petit Malin to notify them that she needed time off to deal with an emergency. It was only afterwards, when she had a chance to reflect, that Tania was struck by the illogicality of the situation: why was Bilodo rushing off to Ségolène?

It seemed absurd. Hadn't he dreaded meeting her so much that he'd preferred suicide? Was he no longer afraid that the Guadeloupian would discover the truth? Did he expect her to welcome him with open arms? The opposite appeared much more probable; seeing that she was dealing with an impostor, Ségolène would be unable to trust Bilodo and would reject him – the best possible outcome for Tania, who would then need only to gather up the fragments of his broken heart.

In actual fact, it wasn't possible to foresee what the Guadeloupian woman's reaction might be. It would all depend on the story Bilodo told her. Was he going to wrap himself in a new web of lies? Would she let herself be moved? The only thing that was absolutely certain was that Bilodo was flying to Ségolène, and that Tania could do nothing about it.

Or maybe there *was* something: hadn't she saved the Guadeloupian's email address?

18

As he stepped out of the airport, Bilodo was struck by the heat and by the contrast between the universe he'd left behind and the one he'd just entered, such as the royal palms above his head that had replaced the frozen streetlights of Montreal. He got into a taxi and gave the driver Ségolène's address. The city wasn't far away, but the taxi soon had to come to a stop because a parade featuring costumed musicians and dancers was blocking one of the main roads. The driver explained that they were celebrating the last day of Carnival. 'Tonight we burn Vaval,' he said, sounding his horn in vain while the procession of brightly dressed revellers showed no sign of coming to an end.

Bilodo knew what was going on. He had visited Guadeloupe only in spirit, but in his efforts to learn all he could about the natural setting in the heart of which Ségolène glittered like a gem in a jewellery case, he'd read a great deal about the island region and educated himself in many of its aspects, including the local customs. As luck would have it, he had flown to *l'île Papillon*, the 'Butterfly Island', on Ash Wednesday, a highlight of the cultural calendar. That very evening, the last day of Carnival, forty days of festivities would culminate with a big *vidé*, a general parade, and everywhere, from Basse-Terre to

Saint-François by way of Pointe-à-Pitre, she-devils in chequered dresses would burn effigies of Vaval, the wicked king of Carnival who symbolized the troubles of the year just passed.

The taxi dropped Bilodo off in front of a white house that faced a square and was surrounded by other, similar dwellings. He hesitated, suddenly confused. He had come to Guadeloupe in order to explain everything to Ségolène and to express the astronomical depths of his love, but here he was, and the words he'd so carefully prepared to achieve his purpose were escaping him. Nevertheless, unable to retreat, he raised a shaking finger to the doorbell...

'It's no use, nobody's home,' said a female voice off to his left.

Bilodo turned and saw an elderly woman, no doubt the neighbour, standing on the other side of a little fence and holding a watering can. Proudly planted in the middle of a bed of dazzlingly coloured flowers, she herself was wearing a dress printed with floral motifs so bright that she perfectly mimicked her environment – which was the reason why Bilodo hadn't immediately noticed her presence. And suddenly he remembered one of Ségolène's haiku:

> My neighbour Aimée
> gardens in a floral dress
> you would water her

'Madame Aimée?' asked Bilodo, taking a chance.

'Do we know each other?' the lady responded, no doubt wondering what planet this peculiar individual in the anorak had come from.

'Ségolène has spoken to me about you,' Bilodo replied, lightly stretching the truth.

'Really?' said Aimée in surprise.

'Would you by chance know where she is?'

'Yes, I know where she is. Where else would she be at this hour? She's at work, of course.'

'Of course,' Bilodo repeated. 'And what's the name of the school where she teaches?'

'Fernande-Bonchamps Public School.'

'Thanks,' he said hurriedly, leaving Aimée to her flowers and dashing off in search of another taxi.

At the Fernande-Bonchamps school, the head teacher informed Bilodo that Ségolène was unavailable. Then, concerned for the security of his staff, the teacher asked Bilodo to identify himself as well as the reason for his visit.

'It's urgent and personal,' Bilodo declared, producing his passport.

'Very well,' the educator said after examining the document. 'Madame Ségolène is at the Mamelles park.'

'At the what?' asked Bilodo, nonplussed. The teats park?

'At the Parc National des Mamelles, over on

Basse-Terre,' the educator explained. 'She took a group of pupils there on a field trip.'

Bilodo rented a Peugeot and followed the GPS directions. Indifferent to the stunning landscape filing past all around him, he crossed a mountainous region and then entered the Mamelles park, whose name no doubt referred to the round shapes of the surrounding hills. Bilodo parked his car near a school bus. At the ticket window, he learned that the park contained both a zoo and a botanical garden. He paid the admission fee and then ventured along the paths of a forest resembling a jungle, with flower-laden branches and a mingling of perfumes that made him giddy. Bilodo climbed a path lined with orchids and reached a belvedere, a vast esplanade overlooking a panorama of hills whose lush green backs overlapped one another all the way to the Caribbean Sea. There were about a hundred visitors on the belvedere, including some fifty schoolchildren in uniform, gathered around two adult guides. One of them was Ségolène.

There she was, an angelic apparition in a simple white dress. Surrounded by children to whom she was giving a lesson in natural science, she spoke in a clear, lilting voice that to Bilodo's ears sounded like heavenly music. Ségolène was magnificently there, letting the universe gravitate around her as if that were normal, so near and yet as inaccessible as if she were a thousand kilometres away from the petrified Bilodo. Overawed to the marrow, he sat down on a bench. He judged himself unworthy of her and hardly dared to lift his eyes. Now, so close to his goal, Bilodo realized that the task of confessing everything to Ségolène exceeded his powers. Where could he find the courage to look her in the face without dying of shame? How could he even approach her without faltering? Was he going to remain where he was, unable to make a move, trapped, tormented, writhing inside? Would he take root in that bench, an oversized bonsai slowly but surely colonized by lichen?

A quiet sound – a sort of droning – attracted Bilodo's attention. Raising his eyes, he saw a hummingbird with iridescent feathers. Hardly bigger than a thumb, the hummingbird was hovering in front of an orchid as if suspended on a wire. Thrusting its tongue into the flower's corolla, the bird gathered the nectar while beating its phantom-like wings at supersonic speed. It was a gripping spectacle, almost too true to be real. At the completion of its nectar feast, the hummingbird bowed reverently to the flower and then disappeared into the forest, leaving Bilodo with the impression of having admired a living haiku...Suddenly inspired, he pulled out his pen. Bending over the brochure he'd been given at the entrance to the park, he wrote:

Of all these orchids
I swear you're the loveliest
hummingbird's honour

It was surely the best way to re-establish contact after such a long silence. That makeshift haiku would revive Ségolène's memory of their epistolary joys; nothing could better dispose her to hear what Bilodo had to say. But it was still necessary to find a way of placing the poem before her eyes. Preferring to remain invisible, Bilodo spotted a schoolboy with an impish face and motioned him closer. He charged the boy with handing the haiku to his teacher and gave him a coin for his trouble. As soon as the child had turned his back on him, Bilodo scurried into the forest and hid behind a giant fern so that he could watch without being seen. The schoolboy, carrying out his mission, brought the brochure to Ségolène, who read the poem. Visibly flabbergasted, she questioned the young messenger, who pointed at the bench, now empty, where Bilodo had been sitting a moment before. Ségolène scrutinized the surroundings. Hidden behind his foliage screen, Bilodo was in a position to ascertain that the beautiful Guadeloupian was in a state of great agitation. She seemed to be as overwhelmed as he was.

Bilodo followed the bus that took the young field-trippers back to their school; then he waited in his car, keeping an eye on the entrance. Now he was feeling fairly strong, ready to present himself to Ségolène. He would confess the fraud he'd felt constrained to perpetrate, and he would justify his conduct by invoking the love he had borne for Ségolène ever since the first haiku. He would declare that he belonged to her, that he wanted to marry her, and that he wished to live with her right there in Guadeloupe.

Twenty minutes later, Ségolène appeared. She had unbound her hair, which floated freely down to her shoulders – a wild mane the wind wrapped itself in. Going on foot, she entered a maze of narrow streets. Bilodo left his car and followed her at a distance.

It was a lively neighbourhood. Numerous residents were wearing Carnival costumes, which allowed Bilodo to melt into the background without too much difficulty. Entering the great hall of the Saint-Antoine market, Ségolène made her way among the multicoloured, fragrant stalls, with their heaps of fruits, vegetables, syrups and spices, their parakeets, brooms and potions reputed to cure all the illnesses in the world. With graceful movements, she weighed a *carambola* in her hand, selected some *figue-pomme* bananas, and then negotiated the price of a bunch of parsley. She didn't look as serene as she did in Bilodo's dreams: guessing that she was being spied on, she frequently looked about her. The schoolboy had no doubt described for her the author of the hummingbird haiku; she knew that it couldn't be Grandpré and had to wonder uneasily who her unknown admirer was and how he knew about her fondness for Japanese poetry.

Her purchases made, Ségolène left the market, walking so fast that Bilodo nearly lost her in the crowd. He tailed her with increased vigilance and soon recognized the square near to where she lived. On this early evening, the place was filled with playing children, and also with adults allowing themselves a moment of crepuscular relaxation. Ségolène crossed the park. Eager to make himself known before she reached her home, Bilodo shortened the distance that separated them. But when he was only a few steps behind Ségolène, two little boys came running up to her; she stopped, bent down, and embraced them both affectionately. Bilodo froze, trying to make himself believe that those were two little neighbours of hers, and she was only their friend or perhaps their favourite babysitter. Then a tall Guadeloupian man stood up from a nearby bench, walked over to Ségolène, and kissed her with unequivocal tenderness. Had a lightning bolt struck Bilodo at that moment, he would not have been more efficaciously zapped. 'She's married! The mother of two children!' he said to himself in despair, horrified by that sweet familial tableau, which to his eyes looked rather like Bosch's *Hell*.

Daddy picked up the little boys, pleased to tote that fidgety, laughing load home. Before following them, Ségolène turned around, prompted by some instinct, and saw Bilodo standing before her like a statue. Their eyes locked. Bilodo had the impression of plunging directly into Ségolène's soul, of instantaneous familiarity, of knowing all she was. And he felt that it was mutual, that she too could see his deepest nature, that he was naked before her, and that she guessed he was the real correspondent, the distant friend, the gentle poetic lover – but also the liar, the usurper, the lunatic. It seemed incredible, but a single look had sufficed to clarify everything between them, without their needing to utter so much as a word.

'I just came...' Bilodo mumbled.

Ségolène stood in what appeared to be a defensive position. He would have liked to reassure her, to say something nice, but his brain was empty. Ségolène glanced at her husband, who was going off with the children; as yet, he hadn't noticed a thing. She turned to Bilodo and addressed him in an imploring voice: 'Please leave. Go away.'

Bilodo inwardly collapsed.

Shouldn't he throw himself at Ségolène's feet and beg her to love him, to follow him with her children, to come and live with him in Montreal?

'Please,' Ségolène said again.

Miraculously, Bilodo managed to get a hold of himself. Knowing that unless he parted from

19

Tania stepped down onto the tarmac at Pointe-à-Pitre International Airport early that evening. She tried to call Bilodo from the taxi, but without success. Having arrived seven hours before her, he'd had all the time he needed to look for – and find – Ségolène. In hindsight, Tania was no longer sure the email she'd sent the Guadeloupian woman had been a good idea. She'd sent it from the airport in Montreal, and in it she'd revealed to Ségolène the truth about Bilodo and warned her of his coming. Informing on him like that had probably resulted in a hostile welcome for Bilodo, who must be furious at her. How would he react when he discovered that she'd followed him to Guadeloupe?

The city was throbbing to the rhythm of the Carnival. Indifferent to such commotion, Tania had the taxi driver drop her off at her hotel, where she immediately refreshed herself in the shower. When she stepped out, a text message was waiting for her – and it had come from Ségolène: 'I got your message. I met your friend Bilodo today. Call me.'

Like voluptuous fruits waiting only to be nibbled: such were Ségolène's lips. The beautiful Guadeloupian

163

was studying a photograph on Tania's phone screen. Bilodo and Tania were smiling in the photo, a 'selfie' she'd taken of them on the Place d'Armes during a recent ramble through Old Montreal.

The two women were sitting at a table in a bistro and had already regaled each other with accounts of the bizarre events that had brought them together at this precise point in time and space. Tania had been astonished to learn that Ségolène was married, that she had children and that she had deceived her husband, committing a certain kind of poetic adultery by correspondence. Ségolène, therefore, was no saint. The icon had a few nicks in it, and so the underlying portrait was exposed, the picture of a woman capable of sin, who was human after all – a revelation that had doubtless been traumatizing for Bilodo, who had suddenly found himself confronted with the impossible. Tania's chances of getting him back had therefore improved, provided that she could find out where he was. On that subject, Ségolène declared herself ignorant: 'I have absolutely no idea where he might have gone after he left me,' she told Tania.

As she was being fascinated by the Guadeloupian's eyes, sparkling like crystal-clear water, Tania finally had to admit that her much-envied rival bore no resemblance whatsoever to an enemy. And what a striking duo they made, the pale Smurfette and the dark, slender island woman. They were, somehow, the two faces of Bilodo's love, brought together against all odds in exceptional circumstances. Meanwhile, Ségolène was still examining the photograph, and she pointed out that they looked happy. Tania contemplated her screen image, arm-in-arm with Bilodo, smiling: yes, they had been happy. For such a brief moment. And she hid her face, for tears threatened to spill from her eyes.

'You love him, don't you?' asked Ségolène, moved by the sight.

'Yes, but the one he loves is you.'

'That's not possible. He doesn't know me.'

'He knows you through your poems.'

'I didn't even know Bilodo existed,' the Guadeloupian protested. 'I thought I was writing to Gaston.'

'You were in love with Gaston Grandpré?'

'I thought I was. But I was mistaken,' Ségolène confessed.

'What do you mean? All those beautiful things you wrote to him, the feelings you claimed to have for him...'

'They were just words. Just poetry.'

'I don't understand,' said Tania, protesting in her turn. 'If you didn't love Grandpré, why did you offer to come to Montreal? What would have been the point of such a long trip?'

Ségolène took a sip of sangria, made a decision, and spoke in a confidential tone: 'I met Gaston on an Internet site dedicated to Japanese poetry, where I'd published a few haiku,' she recounted.

'He contacted me. He said he liked my poems a
lot and started to send me some of his, which I
thought were very beautiful. That was how I got a
Canadian correspondent and our exchange began.
In the beginning, it was nothing but a pleasant literary diversion, like a hobby he and I both enjoyed.
And for a long time it stayed that way, a simple
exchange of poems between friends, right up until
the day when a crisis broke out, last year—'

'A crisis?' said Tania.

'I found out my husband had been cheating on
me with one of my friends. He had put an end to
their relationship before I learned about it, but I
still couldn't accept it; I was hurt, I was outraged.
I couldn't bear his presence any more. I kicked him
out of the house, and there I remained, alone with
my children, and really quite depressed, I have to
say. That was when Gaston's haiku changed. It was
as though he had guessed I was unhappy and wanted to console me. As though he was trying to get
closer to me. In any case, the tone of his poems was
different.'

'I'm sure that happened when Bilodo took
Grandpré's place and started writing to you. It never
occurred to you that a different person was composing the haiku?'

'Never. I was a little surprised, but I got caught
up in the game, and it wasn't long before our *renku* became more intimate. Those poems comforted
me, they inspired me. They were so passionate...I let

myself get carried away. I wanted to believe in that new love, that second chance. I saw it as an opportunity to start my life over in Canada. That was why I planned to travel to Montreal. I was eager to see for myself if it would really be possible between us, and I wanted to let Gaston know that I was the mother of two young children. I wrote to him to announce my intention, but...'

'He didn't reply,' said Tania, completing her sentence.

'I didn't know it was Bilodo I was dealing with, and of course I knew nothing about his accident. I thought I was writing to Gaston. His silence troubled me – I interpreted it as a rejection. I figured he didn't want to make a commitment to me. I told myself I'd gone too far and frightened him. I truly regretted sending him that tanka! But I didn't want to impose on him. I respected his desire to break off our connection; I resigned myself to losing him.'

'That couldn't have been easy,' Tania said sympathetically, well remembering her own distress of the previous spring.

'There were some hard moments,' Ségolène acknowledged. 'But it all turned out positive in the end. I was forced to put my feet back on the ground and see that I was neglecting the essential thing: my family. My children needed me. Their father was begging me to take him back. I found the strength to forgive him, and I let him come back to the house, just before Christmas. Aurélien's a good father. It will never again be the way it was between us, but we've made up. My children suffered from our separation, and I don't want that to happen again. We've gone back to the pleasure of living together, all four of us.'

'I'm happy for you,' Tania said sincerely.

'Do you believe Bilodo could be dangerous?' Ségolène asked, looking worried. 'He wouldn't try to destroy my family, would he?'

Tania assured her that Bilodo was harmless. But to tell the truth, who could guess what was currently stewing in that overheated head? Tania turned on her smartphone and checked Bilodo's credit-card account. She saw that he had neither got back on a plane nor reserved a hotel. Unless Bilodo had swum away from Guadeloupe, he must still be slinking about somewhere, no doubt disoriented. She tried in vain to call him. Ségolène scared up a phone directory and they systematically went through the list of hotels in Pointe-à-Pitre, dialling each one in turn on Tania's phone. But the fugitive's name didn't appear on any register. 'What shall we do?' Tania wondered. Inform the police that there was a Montrealer in distress wandering around their city and possibly considering some nefarious plan? Call the hospitals? Inquire at the morgue?

'I have to find him,' she decided.

Ségolène offered to go with her.

They started by exploring the neighbourhood around the port. This was a hot spot on that evening, the final opportunity for festivities before the beginning of Lent. The streets were packed with night prowlers, to whom Ségolène spoke in Antillean Creole while Tania showed them the Place d'Armes selfie on her smartphone screen, pointing at Bilodo. Having covered the harbour basin from one end to the other, the two women headed for Place de la Victoire, where the Carnival activities were now concentrating and the commotion reaching its climax. Frenzied dancers escorted a great effigy of the villainous Vaval to the stake. In the crush of people around the procession, Tania thought she caught a glimpse of Bilodo and charged, but it was only a French tourist who looked a little like him. Continuing their progress through the jubilant crowd like persistent ants, the two women turned down several invitations to *zouker* – to dance the *zouk* – and showed the photograph to anyone willing to look. But no one recognized Bilodo.

Shortly before midnight, with the horrible Vaval already ablaze, Tania and Ségolène, somewhat discouraged, ended up on the steps of the statue of Félix Éboué. Ségolène's telephone rang. It was Aurélien, her husband, worried about her being out on a night dedicated to wild public behaviour.

'I'm going to have to go home,' she said to Tania.

'I have my class tomorrow morning.'

Tania, who had been awake for thirty-six hours, felt suddenly exhausted. The probability of finding Bilodo this way – wandering about at random – appeared infinitesimal, and she decided to suspend her search for the time being. Ségolène expressed regret at not having been able to help Tania any further and accompanied her back to her hotel. Tania apologized for having dragged Ségolène into that senseless adventure.

'It wasn't your fault,' Ségolène replied. 'You just worry about Bilodo, and keep me up to date on what happens, won't you?'

The Guadeloupian woman kissed Tania like a sister and then got into a taxi. Touched, Tania watched the taxi drive away. She went into the hotel and entered her room.

'Just one word, nothing more, I'm begging you,' Tania texted Bilodo, without real conviction and moreover without result. She got into bed. Unable to shut her eyes, she listened to the noises of Carnival that slipped into the room through the partly open window.

The hands of the clock guillotined the minutes implacably, and Tania turned round in her sheets, haunted by the fear that Bilodo might have committed some self-destructive act. An image obsessed her, the noose swaying from the ceiling of Grandpré's apartment...

'Grandpré?' she suddenly thought.

Tania got out of bed. She went down to the reception desk, borrowed a telephone book and once again picked though the list of hotels in Pointe-à-Pitre, calling each one and asking, this time, to speak to a guest named Gaston Grandpré.

Fortune smiled on her with the seventeenth call.

20

It was still night when Tania presented herself at the Midas Hotel, an establishment unworthy of the starry firmament. A comatose employee gave her the number of the room occupied by Gaston Grandpré.

Wondering what could have impelled Bilodo once again to borrow the identity of the man with the red carnation, Tania went up to his room and listened at the door. She heard nothing. She dared to give the door a few light raps. Still nothing. The door wasn't locked. Warily venturing into the semi-darkness of a shabby room that stank of alcohol and vomit, Tania inadvertently kicked an empty bottle and sent it rolling across the floor. She discovered Bilodo on the bed. He was lying in his own ejecta, alive but unconscious. Tania opened the balcony door to ventilate the decadent scene a little and then bent over Bilodo, who really didn't look very good. He refused to wake up. Seeing that he was feverish, Tania went to get him some water.

Later, having cooled Bilodo down somewhat, Tania texted Ségolène to tell her that she had found the runaway. Ségolène replied a little while later, asking Tania to keep her informed. But there was nothing very agreeable to report; Bilodo opened his eyes from time to time, but he never truly regained consciousness – he would stammer some incoherent words, vomit and then pass out again.

All through the morning, and then all day long, Tania looked after Bilodo, bathing his temples with cool water, wiping his burning forehead, stoically bearing the stifling heat that prevailed in the non-air-conditioned hotel. In the evening, Bilodo's fever suddenly got worse. He was delirious, babbling disjointedly about orchids and hummingbirds. Perhaps taking Tania for Ségolène, Bilodo seized her wrist and mumbled something that sounded like a haiku. Then some violent cramps bent him double. He went rigid, convulsed like one of the strung-out heroin addicts Tania had seen in a television documentary. Bilodo's condition grew so alarming that she considered calling the emergency services, but after a few moments he began to relax, and little by little he grew calm. His fever fell and he dozed off and was soon resting peacefully. Reassured, Tania allowed herself a quick shower. Then she lay down next to Bilodo, resolved to watch over him as long as her strength held out.

Grandpré was sitting at his favourite table in the Madelinot, wearing his red kimono. With studied movements, he poured himself some tea and said:

> Swirling like water
> against rugged rocks,
> time goes around and around

Why was he reciting that haiku, which Bilodo knew
only too well? Grandpré savoured his tea, displaying
a wise smile, and...Bilodo opened his eyes. Hanging
from the ceiling, a lazy fan laboured to stir the air.
Bilodo found himself lying on a damp bed, in a
suffocating room. He didn't know how he'd ended
up in such a place. By dint of a mental effort, he
remembered that he had run, that he had wept, that
he had run for a long time while weeping. Then he'd
walked about at random, stumbling amid the smok-
ing wreckage of his foolish romantic ambitions.

> Fare thee well my lucky star
> my too lovely love
> fare thee well my life

Bilodo had meandered through the festive streets
of Pointe-à-Pitre, feeling only desolation. As for the
tropical setting, which had so charmed him when he
dreamily pictured Ségolène in it, he had found it to be,
in reality, horrifying. Losing his way in the twists and
turns of the Carnival, he had taken a drink from every
bottle that was handed to him, he'd sung, shouted and
drunk some more, to the point of heavy intoxication.
He remembered attending Vaval's blazing combus-
tion. He had even danced around the stake, wiggling

to the rhythm of the drums and the cries of '*Vaval kité nou!*' chanted by the ecstatic crowd. Bilodo, aware that the incineration symbolized the purification of the soul, had envied the ignoble Vaval, who in spite of his uncountable sins was nonetheless granted a spontaneous redemption. Bilodo remembered finding this unfair, and wishing that the flames of expiation would consume him rather than Vaval, he had tried to throw himself into the conflagration, but someone – a reveller less wasted than the others? A guardian angel? – had stopped him. After that, everything became foggy: the images were blurred, distorted. Fleeing like Dr Caligari into an expressionistic night, Bilodo had lost his balance and toppled over into a world where nothing was solid...

Someone had asked him for his name and his passport. The principal at the Fernande-Bonchamps school? No, this was much later, at the hotel reception desk. His passport, no longer in his pocket, had been lost or stolen. As for his name...he was obliged to acknowledge that he couldn't remember it. 'Who am I?' he'd guffawed, finding his inability to respond to such an elementary question vastly amusing. Then, in a mirror fastened to the wall in the reception area, he had spotted the reflection of a face he recognized at once – nothing more normal, because it was his own – the familiar, bearded face of a ghost who was none other than himself. 'My name is Gaston Grandpré,' he'd declared, placing on the counter a fistful of dollars.

A sensation of movement yanked Bilodo out of that spectral memory. The bed creaked, the mattress shifted slightly, and he perceived that he wasn't alone. A woman was asleep at his side, her back turned to him. A woman who wasn't Ségolène, because her hair was blonde, because her skin was as white as mother-of-pearl. It was Tania, dressed only in knickers and a camisole. How had she come to be beside him? And what were the two of them doing in that bed?

Stunned, Bilodo got up slowly so as not to wake Tania, stepped into the little bathroom, and locked himself in. Suddenly feeling intensely thirsty, he drank from the tap and then rinsed out his mouth for a long time, trying to get rid of a foul aftertaste. He hardly dared to look at himself in the mirror, afraid of seeing Grandpré's face, but the dead man did not appear, probably because he was busy in some other corner of the Great Beyond. Bilodo went back into the bedroom. Tania was still sleeping. Shouldn't he seize his chance and get out of there? Looking at the young woman, he was surprised to find he didn't hate her. In fact, he wasn't even cross with her. The anger Tania's duplicity had aroused in him had inexplicably vanished. Bilodo was amazed at how magnanimous he felt. Feeling the need for some fresh air, he walked out onto the little balcony, which overlooked the port.

A pleasant breeze was blowing in off the sea. It was early. Bilodo's thoughts drifted towards

Ségolène, marked with a serenity that ultimately disconcerted him. How could he be thinking of her with such detachment, as though their love story were ancient history? The crazy day he'd spent pursuing Ségolène from one end of Guadeloupe to the other, all the way to the final shock of their meeting – all that seemed like part of a previous life. What had become of the passion that had carried him to her over land and sea? What was it that had gone on inside him?

Everything that had happened to Bilodo since the fragrance of the lemons revived his memory now seemed to have little more consistency than a dream. And that, he realized in a sudden flash of lucidity, was exactly the point: Ségolène's love had been only a dream, a dream from which he had just – finally – awakened.

Ségolène had never loved him. Nor he her, for that matter, not really. He had practised self-delusion, desiring at all costs to believe he was in love, but in reality loving only love itself. The whole thing had been no more than a mirage, a sublime fantasy, an irresistible obsession he'd felt compelled to go all the way to the end of, crossing over the border into madness, rushing ahead faster and faster until he lost control and veered off the rails. And now that he was entirely consumed, poor little Vaval, and was being reborn, purified, from his ashes – now that he was seeing the world with new eyes – the person he found at his side was Tania.

Bilodo stepped back into the room. Tania was still sleeping, and he thought she looked even more beautiful than she had on that recent night when he'd entered her bedroom and gazed at her for a long time while she slept. It was as if time were making one of those poetic loops so dear to Grandpré's heart, bringing Bilodo back to that precise mental point, that moment of nocturnal adoration in Tania's room, back when he still remembered nothing and was totally ignorant of her treachery. She had deceived him, certainly, but not more monstrously than he'd fooled himself, and basically for the same reason – for love – that was why she'd followed him, it was why she was there, in that crummy bed, despite everything that Bilodo had put her through.

Ségolène's love had been only a dream, but Tania's was genuine; Bilodo could see that now, and this essential realization dynamited the last dike around his heart, releasing a torrent of emotions. As he gazed at the sleeping Tania, he admired her finely drawn lips, the harmonious curve of her hip, the delicate roundness of her small toes, and he marvelled at finding her so beautiful, so extraordinarily real.

Tania twitched in her sleep and rolled over on her back. The movement pushed up her camisole, which tightened across her breasts and revealed her navel, surrounded by golden down. Spellbound at seeing her offered like that, Bilodo stiffened...

Tania was having a very exciting dream. She dreamt that she and Bilodo were making love. The sensations were intense. Everything was vivid, everything was acute; incredibly realistic, this erotic dream of hers. So much so that Tania suddenly began to doubt whether it was a dream, and at the moment when her pleasure reached its culmination, she became aware that she wasn't sleeping, that she was awake – and that it was indeed him!

At seven thirty-six that morning, seismographs recorded a slight earth tremor on Guadeloupe; the epicentre was the neighbourhood around the port in Pointe-à-Pitre. Hundreds of dogs barked in chorus, and thousands of pigeons took flight simultaneously, while clouds of panic-stricken bats streamed out of belfries and attics, briefly darkening the sky. Some citizens became alarmed, imagining they were reading the signs of an imminent eruption of La Soufrière – a catastrophe which, however, did not take place. Few people would make the connection between those various incidents and another, equally unusual phenomenon; dozens of dolphins and three little whales ventured into the waters of the port, swam around in the harbour basin and frolicked right below the quays, drawn in from the open sea by nobody knew what. Fourteen metres away, in room 306 in the terrific Hôtel Midas, Tania was sobbing for joy in the arms of Bilodo, who was crying too.

21

As soon as they returned from Guadeloupe, Tania and Bilodo made haste to inaugurate the bed they had never yet shared. And they made love, insatiably, pausing only to talk of what was happening to them, of all the happiness raining down upon them, of what they knew and didn't know about each other. To satisfy Tania's curiosity, Bilodo described the bizarre psychological process by which he had transformed himself into Gaston Grandpré's double, the one she'd met on the balcony at the end of August: 'You saved my life twice that day. The first time was when your visit stopped me from hanging myself, and the second was after the accident, when you revived me,' he concluded, enriching his testimony with all the proofs of gratitude that Tania could desire.

The next day, they went to Noémie's to fetch Bill and found him in the company of a charming female congener with prominent eyes. By way of helping Bill stave off boredom, Noémie had procured him a girlfriend, a situation about which he seemed as happy as a fish in water. Noémie invited the two lovers to take advantage of her chalet in the Laurentides and even offered to lend them her car. Tania and Bilodo accepted, unable to conceive a better way to end the winter, and the following day they drove north to that log cabin in the midst of the untamed wilderness.

The chalet was, in the words of an old song, the perfect '*cabane au Canada*', buried in snow. They intended to make the most of the great outdoors and go skiing and take long walks on snowshoes under the trees, but actually they dedicated most of their time to indoor sports. Tania could think of nothing that would increase her happiness, and had nothing more to wish for, other than that nobody would come and disturb their tranquillity: she just wanted the sweet moments of the existence they were spending together in that fairytale realm of snow to go on and on and never change. And so, until the end of February, they made love without restraint, and with so much passion that the chalet became the epicentre of a localized climate change, in the form of a precocious little early spring that made the snow melt and the flowers sprout within a radius of fifteen metres.

March arrived on the sly. For Bilodo, the time had come to go back to being the postman he had never stopped being deep down inside. Tania bowed to necessity, regretful at leaving the snug nest they'd made for themselves in the heart of the Laurentides, but at the same time seeing no reason to fear their return to Montreal, because she no longer had anything to hide.

It was a joy for Bilodo to put on his uniform again. He had been assigned his old route in Saint-Janvier, and when he stepped into the Madelinot at noon on his first day back, he was surprised to see behind the counter none other than Tania, whom Mr Martinez had rehired without hesitation. The amused couple pretended to be as shy as in former days and much enjoyed this little historical reconstruction, even though it was incomplete; after all, certain principal actors were missing, such as Grandpré, the man with the red carnation, and Robert, who had been transferred to another district.

Bilodo was glad to be working again, and Tania was in a position to ascertain that he committed no postal indiscretions; undoubtedly, he no longer felt the need to live by appropriating another's existence. The happiness of their great romance seemed so perfect that it made Tania uneasy; she didn't dare surrender herself to the whims of a destiny that had so often knocked her about. Was Bilodo really over Ségolène? He declared that she no longer counted in his eyes, but her feeling of uneasiness was stronger than herself; she couldn't help obscurely dreading the eventual arrival of a citrus-scented letter. Bilodo swore there was no room in his heart for anyone but Tania, and to prove he meant what he said, he resolved to destroy the haiku: that would convince her beyond a shadow of a doubt that Ségolène belonged to the past.

They picked up the box containing the haiku from Noémie's apartment, and when they got home, Bilodo made a fire in the hearth. The first documents he took out of the box were the book contract Tania had neglected to sign and the manuscript of Grandpré's volume of haiku, *Enso*. Examining the collection, Bilodo appeared mesmerized by the black circle that illustrated its first page.

'Is something wrong?' Tania asked.

'This word, *Enso*...'

'The title of the collection?'

'It was the last word I spoke before I died,' Bilodo revealed.

'*Enso*? What does it mean?'

'I've been intrigued by this word ever since the first time I saw it. I did some research. It's a Japanese word, and it refers to this circle here on the cover of the manuscript,' he explained.

Bilodo went on to say that the *Enso* circle was a traditional symbol in Zen Buddhism, representing the emptiness of mind which alone allows one to attain enlightenment. Having been painted by Zen masters for centuries, that circle, drawn with a single, continuous brushstroke, prompted a spiritual exercise in meditation on nothingness and revealed the artist's state of mind: one could produce a powerful, well-balanced *Enso* only when one's mind was clear, liberated from all thought or intention. Bilodo added that the Zen circle could also represent perfection, truth, infinity, the cycle of the seasons, or the turning wheel. Overall, *Enso* symbolized the loop, the cyclical nature of the universe, history always repeating itself, the perpetual return to the starting point. It was similar in that sense to the Greek ouroboros symbol, depicting a serpent biting its own tail. Bilodo flipped through the pages of Grandpré's manuscript and showed Tania how it ended with the same haiku that had begun it:

> Swirling like water
> against rugged rocks,
> time goes around and around

Tania recognized that such a duplication couldn't be accidental. That final echo of the first poem, which moreover evoked a circular image, and that title, *Enso*, unquestionably invited the reader to a perpetual rereading of the work. But what did any of that have to do with Bilodo's accident?

'Why did you say that word before you...lost consciousness?'

Bilodo's pupils reflected the fire in the hearth as he related how he had died that day. How, in his haste to post the haiku in which he invited Ségolène to come to Montreal, he had run out into the storm and dashed across the street towards the postbox, which Robert was hurriedly emptying of its contents, and...Bilodo hadn't seen the truck coming. He remembered only the sound of a horn, followed by a terrible shock and unbearable pain. At the end of a blurry moment, he'd seen Robert bending over him. Then a second face appeared – another post-man, accompanying Robert – equally familiar, but for a completely different reason; he had Bilodo's own face. The face of the Bilodo that he had been: a perfect double of himself...What witchcraft had left him stretched out on the asphalt and at the same time hovering aloft, observing himself? The answer had come to him like an interior voice, whispering the haiku that began and concluded Grandpré's collection:

> Swirling like water
> against rugged rocks,
> time goes around and around

And then Bilodo had understood. That was exactly what was going on. He had become Grandpré – a second Grandpré, caught in a metaphysical trap that made time whirl around and the past do loops. How could the similarities to Grandpré's fatal accident of the previous year be ignored? Hadn't he, Bilodo, even been holding a letter addressed to Ségolène that had slipped from his fingers and been swallowed by the storm drain, just like the one that got away from Grandpré?

Obviously, that was all absurd. In retrospect, Bilodo realized that it could only have been a hal-lucination – that his double had been nothing more than an illusion, a consequence of the trauma he'd just suffered. Quite obviously, there had never been any temporal loop or metaphysical trap or other evil spell. And yet, he remembered, at the moment of his dying he had found the whole thing perfectly logical, he had truly believed that he'd turned into Grandpré, the man with whom he had so strongly wished to identify. And so it was with the conviction of being condemned to perpetuate the hellish destiny of an eternally repeated death that he had breathed his last, uttering that fateful word: *Enso*...

Bilodo fell silent. Entranced by his story, Tania jumped when he suddenly burst into unexpected laughter: 'It's incredible to think a person could imagine such foolishness,' he said, laughing hard.

Bilodo took up the contract for the publication of the poetry collection *Enso*, produced a pen, and signed the document, imitating Grandpré's signature. As for the rest, the papers and all the poems, he burned them in the fireplace.

Tania married Bilodo early in July, at City Hall in Montreal. Present were Noémie and Mr Martinez, who acted as witnesses, as well as the itinerant Ulysse, who wished them the endless posterity of Olympian demigods.

That very evening, the young newlyweds boarded a flight to Munich, setting off on a three-week honeymoon in Bavaria. For Bilodo it was the opportunity to meet his parents-in-law, Bernhard and Hildegard Schumpf, as well as the other members of his new German family-by-marriage. Proud to serve as his guide, Tania introduced Bilodo to her corner of her native country, revealing to him its unsuspected charms in the process and providing him with many occasions to go into raptures. As anticipated, Uncle Reinhardt placed his country house at the couple's disposal; this dwelling, which seemed to have sprung straight out of one of the Grimm brothers' fairytales, hoisted its eccentric gables under the vigilant guard of centuries-old pine trees. It was there that they spent the most unforgettable moments of their journey, on the shores of Lake Starnberg, that twinkling sapphire set in the Alps, where the young Sisi, the future Empress of Austria, had canoed and fished in former days, and on whose margins, long afterwards, little Tania had so often dreamt that she was Romy Schneider.

22

The young couple had been back in Montreal for several weeks when Tania, doing some errands on a fine morning in late August, received an unexpected telephone call from Madame Brochu. The lady had just found on her doorstep a package, delivered in her absence and addressed to Gaston Grandpré. Not knowing what to do with it, she was seeking advice from Tania, who had so conscientiously disposed of the deceased's other effects. Rue des Hêtres was nearby; half an hour later, with Madame Brochu looking on, Tania opened the package, which contained twenty freshly printed copies of the haiku collection *Enso*, presented with the publisher's compliments. On the cover of this little volume there was a depiction of the ouroboros, the serpent biting its tail, an illustration that Tania deemed germane to the poet's enterprise – Grandpré would have been pleased.

Madame Brochu was delighted to get rid of those strange books, and Tania found herself on the pavement with twenty copies of *Enso*. Knowing that Bilodo's postal route would bring him to rue des Hêtres shortly before noon, she felt an urge to give him a surprise. She called him up and invited him to have lunch with her in the café across the street – the one where she had kept watch, in vain, for the arrival of Ségolène the previous September. Tania took a seat on the terrace near the street, ordered a cup of tea, and waited for Bilodo while perusing Grandpré's haiku.

> At the young waiters'
> big annual race:
> a speaker and a streaker

> Fun in the city
> and sagacity –
> between them a saga lies

> Lost in the miles of
> supermarket aisles
> a weeping, terrorized child

> Magnificent sweep
> Oh! The utter perfection
> of that golfer's swing!

The preceding autumn, Tania had leafed through the manuscript of Grandpré's collection only superficially, stopping now and then to look more closely; but it was a totally different experience to read the poems slowly and in the particular order the author had desired, an arrangement that bestowed on them a sort of incantatory power:

Sitting on the edge
of a new-dug grave
the old man is playing chess

Congested subway
platforms hot jam-packed
with upright, bipedal crabs

The night gets thicker
throttling the moon and
assassinating the stars

The darkness is where
adversaries fight
the most ferocious battles

To break through the horizon
look behind the set
meet and embrace Death

Sombre and yet luminous, the haiku succeeded
one another, a procession of ocean fish exuding
their own phosphorescence. As she turned the pages, Tania had the impression that she was moving
towards an invisible goal, an ineluctable finality. The
haiku resounded, one against the other, producing a
mental music with a haunting rhythm; they elicited
an archetypal sensation of déjà vu, or rather of '*déjà-
rêvé*' – already dreamt. All of a sudden, Tania came
upon this surprising poem:

Lying in the thunderstorm
after the great shock
I breathe my last breath

It was as if Grandpré had foreknown the manner of
his death. Tania wanted to believe that it was just a
coincidence, but believing became difficult when she
read, on the following page,

This thief who steals words
will steal my life too
furtive filcher walking man

That 'walking man', that 'thief who steals words'
– didn't they call to mind a certain inquisitive
postman? Could Grandpré have had a premonition that Bilodo would take his place and assume
his identity, thus 'stealing' his life? But Tania had
seen nothing yet, and her mystification changed
to astonishment when she read the following
poems:

The grieving woman
will stick a red carnation
in the sugar bowl

She loves in secret
He doesn't see her
but adores a distant smile

He shall not perish
from Isis's kiss
it will bring him back to life

How could she see in such verses only a series of coinci-
dences? Tania was compelled to admit that the terribly
familiar story recounted in those haiku was her own.
Having no wish even to try to understand how these
things could be, she kept on reading, recognizing herself, word for word, in the woman Grandpré portrayed:

She'll create for him
a life made of dreams
and obliterate his past

She will dare to confront both
antique demons and
ghosts of the future

She'll cross the waters
carried on the wind
right to the ends of the earth

Far away, where day
and night are mingled
upon a butterfly's back

Her love will prevail
for the length of a wing-flap
just before the storm

And then she will know
the future already was
and will be again

Nothing is born nothing dies
nothing's unchanging
but movement itself

There's no avoiding
the wheel of fortune
and its eternal turning

Swirling like water
against rugged rocks,
time goes around and around

Tania closed the book, silencing its prophecies from beyond the grave. She noticed that she was shaking. In the street before her, the wind bit its own tail, making whirlwinds of newspaper scraps and dead leaves. Tania saw that the sky was black and heavy with clouds. A storm was threatening. Again troubled by a feeling of déjà vu, she suddenly realized...She realized that today was 'the day'. That it was exactly two years ago, two years to the day, that Grandpré had perished – and one year ago, to the day, when an identical death had very nearly carried off Bilodo, on that very street, in the very place where she'd just arranged to meet him.

A thunderclap crashed over Tania's head. The heavens opened and torrential rain began to pour down, and she realized that the past was going to repeat itself and that time, swirling like water against rocks, was preparing to make a new loop. She grabbed her telephone and called Bilodo to warn him, to entreat him to stay far away from rue des Hêtres. But he didn't answer.

The downpour became diluvial. Leaving the protection of the terrace awning, Tania ran down the flooded pavement. She was making a dash for the end of the street, the direction from which Bilodo would probably come. When she didn't see him, she stopped, drenched to the bone, and turned back. Suddenly she saw Bilodo, against all expectation, coming out of the narrow street that ran along the side of Madame Brochu's house. Tania tried to attract his attention by making big gestures and yelling at the top of her voice, but the thunder drowned her out. Bilodo stepped off the pavement and started to cross the street, heading for the café. That was when the truck appeared.

That truck, arriving out of nowhere, going too fast, blasting through the storm. It was going to pass right in front of Tania, and then it would smash into Bilodo in the middle of the street...

Tania took off.

She heard the blare of a horn. Then there was a crash. The world spun, in slow motion, as in a film. Tania whirled around in space, then there was another crash, and the world became steady again, hard beneath her back. The sky flashed, pelted her eyes with rain. She attempted to move, but found she couldn't. A figure slipped in front of the storm. It was Bilodo, horrified, bending over her, silently crying out things she didn't hear. Tania didn't hear anything at all. And yet she did, but she wasn't really 'hearing', she was listening to her inner voice: 'And what are you doing there, Tania Schumpf, lying in the street in that man's place? Don't you fear death?' But no fear dwelled in Tania. She wasn't afraid, for at last she understood – for now she knew that everything had proceeded with implacable logic, that it was the natural movement of a clockwork mechanism she herself had set in motion by saving Bilodo's life when he was destined to perish. By doing so, she had broken the temporal loop in which he was imprisoned, unwittingly initiating the creation of a new loop that could be closed only by her own death. By doing so, she had taken upon herself the curse hanging over Bilodo: it was as simple and terrible as that, and also, in a certain way, as beautiful.

Bilodo took Tania in his arms and spoke mute words she could only guess at by trying to read his lips. How she regretted having to leave him already, after only a few months of happiness. She would have liked to live longer by his side and lavish on him more of the infinite tenderness she harboured in her heart. She would have wished to give him a child, a little Bilodo or a little Tania, who would have climbed the stairs of Vieux-Québec with them, counting the steps for fun, without ever being scared of wicked cable cars. None of that would happen. And yet, serenely did Tania accept her end, joyfully did she consent to that sacrifice, provided that Bilodo could be saved.

Would he know she had died for him? Would he remember their beautiful love for a long time? Might he come now and again and place a carnation on her grave?

Bilodo was weeping. Tania smiled.

'*Enso*,' she whispered as the last breath of life abandoned her.

Acknowledgements

I should like to express my gratitude to Hélène Cummings, Camille Thériault, Aldo Guechi, Jacques Lazure, Maria Vieira, Liedewij Hawke, Hella Reese, Saskia Bontjes van Beek, Richard Roy, Pascal Genêt, Hans-Reinhard and Maren Hörl, Louis Saint-Pierre, Kathy Note and Marc Hendrickx, who helped and supported me throughout the writing of this novel, as well as to Marie Lessard and Daniel Curio of the State of Bavaria Québec Office.

The writing of this novel was made possible thanks to a grant from the Canada Council for the Arts.